ENEMY AT THE GATE

WOMEN OF THE RESISTANCE - BOOK 1

MARY D. BROOKS

AUSXIP PUBLISHING

Edited by: Rosa Alonso
Cover Design: Mary D. Brooks
Interior Design: AUSXIP Publishing

ISBN: 978-0-6485709-3-6

Enemy at the Gate is a work of fiction. All incidents and dialogue, and all characters except for some well-known historical figures, places and events, are products of the author's imagination and are not to be construed as real.

Printed in the United States
AUSXIP Publishing
www.ausxippublishing.com

DEDICATION

*Dedicated to the courageous women
of the Greek Resistance.*

*"When the entire world had lost all hope, the Greek people
dared to question the invincibility of the German monster,
raising against it the proud spirit of freedom."*

-Franklin D Roosevelt, US President 1933 – 1945

ACKNOWLEDGMENTS

Thank you to my incredible editor Rosa Alonso for all her hard work! She is my rock!

Thanks to The Jewish Museum of Greece who gave me unfettered access to their collections and research materials.

Thanks to The Australian War Memorial for their extensive collection of World War 2 research material.

HUGE thanks to my beta-readers, Erin, Danielle and Petra for your feedback and support! It takes a village to birth a novel.

THE HYMN OF LIBERTY (FREEDOM)

Greek National Anthem

English Translation by Rudyard Kipling (1918)
Part of the Greek National Anthem

...

Ah, slow broke that day
And no man dared call,
For the shadow of tyranny
Lay over all:

And we saw thee sad-eyed,
The tears on thy cheeks
While thy raiment was dyed
In the blood of the Greeks.

Yet, behold now thy sons
With impetuous breath
Go forth to the fight
Seeking Freedom or Death.

From the graves of our slain
Shall thy valor prevail
As we greet thee again --
Hail, Liberty! Hail!

CHAPTER 1

MARCH 01, 1941

LARISSA, GREECE - 5 AM

I loved the sound of rain on the roof, jumping in puddles, and the smell of the grass after the rain had stopped. It was clean and felt like the dawn of something better. My name is Zoe Lambros, and I was nearly thirteen years old before everything changed. If you believe in the Fates, you could say that they sealed our futures in the early hours of that soggy first day of March when our long nightmare began. I didn't take any notice of the Fates or anything else for that matter.

It had been raining for most of the week; it was cold, wet, and windy, but no one minded. It had been a brutal winter, mired by the weather and the war against the Italians in the Albanian mountains. We all thought Spring would bring a welcome change; we hadn't had a lot to celebrate since that fateful day in October 1940. We had been plunged into war against the Italians, but our boys were heroically fighting against the invaders, and we were winning. We were confident that they were coming home soon, so convinced that the war was nearly over that we decided it was an excellent time to get baby Arestia christened. She had waited long enough, and if they waited even longer, they would have to have her christening just before her wedding!

It had been quite a party that lasted long into the night. By the time I went to bed, it was around two in the morning.

"Polyxeni wants out! Polyxeni wants out!"

I had barely been asleep for an hour or so when that high-pitched voice penetrated my sleep-deprived brain. I groaned and pulled the blanket over my head in the vain hope the parrot would shut up.

"Polyxeni wants out! Polyxeni wants out!"

"I'm going to kill you, Polyxeni!" I screamed and threw my pillow across the room. Only when it left my hand did it dawn on me that it was a stupid thing to do. Now I had no pillow, and the parrot was still squawking.

"That's not going to shut her up."

"I know something that will…"

"No, don't!"

For a moment, I contemplated ignoring the lump next to me and reaching for my shoes, which were under my bed. My cousin didn't say anything else, so I took it that she had fallen asleep. I should never assume anything, because as I moved to pick up one of the shoes, Arty swiftly rolled on top of me.

"Have you gone deaf?"

I stared up at her and tried my fiercest look. "Get off me before I pull the blanket and you die from the cold!"

As threats went, it was a pathetic one, and my cousin knew it. Arty's green eyes crinkled now that she had finally got the better of me. Arty wasn't her real name–her real name was the glorious-sounding Artemis. Named after our great grandmother, but I would like to believe she was named after the Greek Goddess of the Hunt, of the Amazons, and of the home and women–Goddess Artemis of Mount Olympus, the same Mount Olympus that we could see from Larissa and the tallest mountain in all of Greece.

Her eldest sister was named Maria after our maternal grandmother. Unfortunately, Maria couldn't make it for the christening because she lived on the island of Rhodes with her in-laws. Panos, her husband, was fighting on the Albanian front.

I have five cousins of the same name. The only way we know which Maria we are talking about is when we insert their father's name into the conversation. Greeks are so unimaginative when it comes to names. My parents broke with tradition and called me Zoe. No one else in the family had that name, but to my parents, the name was significant.

I was the last child born to Helena and Nicholas Lambros, and the only daughter after three sons. The story was that my mother nearly lost me before I was born, and there was a great deal of praying to Saint Gregory Palamas to protect me. All that praying worked because my mother carried me to term. I was thrilled they didn't name me Gregoria, in honor of the Saint. They called me Zoe because it means 'life.' There was a great deal of tut-tutting by the family, but they quickly got over it once another Maria was born.

Arty's middle sister was named Elisavet, which is also a regal name. My three cousins were like the sisters I never had; I had three burly brothers and loved them, but they didn't understand me. Arty was six months older than me, and we looked alike–curly red hair, green eyes, and a tendency to speak our minds (not a trait that's appreciated). Elisavet (we called her Ellie), also had the same Mavrakis look; it was like God had decided he didn't want to invent a new look for anyone born of the Mavrakis stock. Our grandmother, Maria, was the source of the red hair and green eyes.

I had a lot of cousins, but only three of them I wanted to spend time with. The rest bored me and made me want to throw something at them. I'm quite sure they didn't think highly of me either. I wasn't interested in their preoccupation with attracting the eye of the boys, their frilly dresses, or their constant gossiping and sticking their noses where they didn't belong. My papa always said that gossip was a sign of unintelligent women. There were a lot of dumb women in this family.

My attention refocused on my predicament. Arty had the good grace to roll off me once the idea of killing the bird had diminished. She settled on her side and smiled. I tried to ignore her superior looking smirk for as long as I could, which wasn't very long.

"Don't kill Polyxeni. Yiayia Maria will be so upset she will die from grief. You want to kill our grandmother?"

"Pappou wanted that bird dead many times!"

"No, he didn't. He was teasing Yiayia…"

"I think your memory is a little faulty. Pappou Stavros asked me for my slippers so he could throw them at the bird!"

Arty stared at me for a moment before she burst out laughing and tried to smother me with a pillow. "You are the craziest girl alive, Zoe Lambros!"

The sound of the rain hitting the roof got louder. My desire to get out of bed evaporated the stronger the rain fell. The parrot was going to live for another day. Polyxeni decided she didn't want to get out of her cage. I think the pillow may have shocked her into silence. Or I may have killed her. I had a quick look and saw the bird was indeed still alive. Next time I wasn't going to miss.

Arty and I dissolved into hysterical giggles when I attempted to steal her pillow from her. We fought for it in a tug-of-war that ended with me falling off the bed and onto the bare wooden floor with a loud thump. That set Polyxeni off again, and we laughed uproariously at the silliness of it all. I got back into bed and snuggled up to Arty so we could share pillow space. It wasn't hard to figure out what she was thinking about now that we had quietened down.

"Uncle Yiannis is an idiot."

Arty didn't say anything, and I thought she wasn't going to discuss my uncle, who had made a spectacle of himself at the party. I can't abide stupid people, especially those I'm related to.

"Idiots can be redeemed, but he's not an idiot; he wanted to wound Mama, and that's all there is to it. He's a vindictive *malarka* who would sell his children if he could. He called her a traitor to her faith, Zoe! I wished someone would take him out in the fields and punch some sense into him."

"You know he doesn't speak for the rest of the family. Ellie will always be Ellie to us, and nothing has changed because she married a Jew and changed her faith."

"It doesn't change how you see Ellie because your parents raised you to believe in family, respect, and honoring others. Yiannis has become a fanatic about the church, and I fear where his fanaticism will lead."

"Yiannis is a coward, and cowards don't act on their hollow words. He's never been the same since he fell off the roof, and there's also his crazy wife. She should have stayed a nun and not marry."

"Falling off a roof doesn't make you a zealot. I'm glad Ellie wasn't here to hear his disrespectful words."

"I think you forget that Ellie can stand up for herself, and she would have put him in his place. I wish that she was with us; I miss her. Hopefully, she can come up next month for your mama's birthday?"

Arty smiled and nodded. "We're planning something huge for Mama, and the whole town will be there."

I smiled inside, knowing I had just changed the subject away from our vile uncle and onto something that was far more enjoyable. I mentally patted myself on the head.

"I know what you're trying to do, Zoe."

Well, that victory was short-lived. I feigned innocence, but that made Arty laugh even more.

"We need another party, and by next month, our boys will be back home as well. We won't invite Yiannis. We have enough village idiots in this family, so we can do without him. Speaking of village idiots, I hope Uncle

Kyriakos stays in America, and we don't see his ugly face. Traitorous–"

"He's not a traitor, Zo. He's just scared."

"We're all scared, but you're not going to see our fathers run like that mad dog. I'm not sure if he is a real Mavrakis. I'm surprised Yiannis has not fled yet. Our families fought together in the Liberation War, and if we go back further in time, I'm quite sure they were Spartan soldiers at Thermopylae."

"Oh, no, don't start about Thermopylae! Please, I beg you, God, make her stop!" Arty put her hand over my mouth and giggled. "You're the only one who talks so much about Thermopylae."

"You mean I'm the only one who knows history?"

"No, just the only one who's obsessed with it."

"I'm not obsessed. I am the family historian. Uncle Kyriakos is not a Spartan. He was born in Grevena. That says everything that needs to be said. Yiannis was also born in Grevena."

"I don't think they are despicable because they were born in Grevena. You weren't born in Sparta either."

"Mama said I was created in Sparta."

Arty's eyes widened before she dissolved into giggles. "Zoe!"

"What? That's what Mama said when I asked her."

"You asked your mother where you were created?"

"No, silly! That would be disgusting. I asked her whether I'm still a Spartan even if I was born in Farsala."

Arty shook her head in apparent disbelief. "Eeew! I'm surprised your mother told you about all of that! My mother would have thrown her slipper at me for daring to ask!"

I had to admit the idea of my parents 'making me' almost made me want to vomit. I was used to seeing my parents kiss, but no, I didn't want to think about all the other stuff. I shook my head to try to clear those mental images. "I think we're going to make ourselves sick if we think about it. Let's not talk about that, or about our stupid uncles. I know something we can talk about..."

"Oh, don't start!" Arty pulled the pillow away from me and hid underneath her blanket.

"He was so sweet, and it was so nice of your mama to invite him! Every time I see him, his hair looks like someone has dunked him in ash, and those crazy black eyes..."

"They're not 'crazy black.'"

"Oh, sorry, I should have said 'eyes like the color of black granite.'" I feigned a swoon and put my hand over my heart, which only made Arty laugh.

"Have you seen how beautiful those eyes are?"

"Yes, he has beautiful eyes. I'm going to be your maid of honor, right?" I wiggled my eyebrows at Arty, which only made her laugh harder.

"You are such a crazy girl, ZoZo."

"He didn't say a word to me for the longest time; I thought he was born mute."

"He's shy, but you eventually got him talking to you. The tall, silent type. I think it's going to be a long courtship."

"I have a book..."

"Oh God, not your romance novels! Whoever gave you those books deserves to be locked in a room with Polyxeni."

"You can take that up with our grandmother! Would you like to be the one to tell her about those terrible books?"

"No, I'm fine, thank you."

"Ha! I thought so. The book is a great idea, cousin. You can learn how to flirt and how to court your young man."

"It's too bad you're not doing that with your boy."

I growled in frustration and pulled the blanket over my head. I was sick of hearing yet another person tell me that a certain boy was sweet on me. "He's not 'my boy.' I don't want to get married."

"He's a good man. You have to get serious about this."

"How did this conversation become about me? You're the one with the boy."

"At least I'm doing something about it."

"I'm thirteen!"

"Grandmother got married at fifteen! My mama got married at sixteen. Yours married at eighteen, and that's old. The war is nearly over, and you have to think about what will happen…"

"He's Athenian."

I was expecting Arty to laugh at me like she usually did when I mentioned my dislike for Athenians. Both the Lambros and the Mavrakis clans were Spartan, hence the question to my mother about my ancestry. I took pride in the knowledge that I don't come from Athenian blood. I wouldn't ever marry an Athenian.

"You really must stop disliking Athenians. They are Greek, just like us."

"They have a funny accent."

"Zoe! Think of all the beautiful babies you will have. His thick black hair and electric blue eyes..."

"Unnatural blue eyes. And how do you get 'electric' blue eyes? Have you seen them up close? Horrible." Yes, I was silly, but I didn't want to be promised in marriage to him. I had different plans for my life. I planned to follow in my mother's footsteps and learn at the best art academy in Athens (even if I didn't like the Athenians, that's where the best schools were). I didn't want to settle down and marry.

"So, you've seen his eyes up close? They are beautiful, and you will be protected against evil spirits as well."

Arty must have been still drunk since she was saying the silliest things. "How will the blue-eyed Athenian protect me?"

"His blue eyes will protect you both from the evil eye, ZoZo!" Arty howled at her joke and almost fell off the bed. That was funny, but I tried not to laugh. The howling was infectious, and we both ended up giggling.

We were still laughing when the door opened, and my mother appeared. I hoped she didn't want me to get out of bed because the last place I wanted to be was outside.

"Polyxeni wants out! Polyxeni wants out!"

"Zoe wants Polyxeni dead! Zoe wants Polyxeni dead!" I mimicked the bird and countered her words every time she asked to fly away. My mother just shook her head at my silliness.

"Mama wants Zoe to get out of bed! Mama wants Zoe to get out of bed!"

Arty and I giggled at my mother's playfulness. "You're so funny, Mama."

"I'm glad you think so. I want you to get up and get

dressed. We have mouths to feed. You need to go to the bakery, and you should take your crossbow in case you find a rabbit along the way, and also stop by Aunty Kaliope's house and see if her hens have laid some eggs."

I wasn't thrilled with the idea of getting up and trudging through the rain. "Mama, we have eggs."

"Don't argue with me, Zoe. Your grandmother's girls haven't laid any this morning, and you know Papa likes to have eggs in the morning. Don't make a face. Come on, get up. Arty, there is work for you too. Up you get!"

How on earth did my mother know I was making a face when I had the blanket over my head? The woman had extraordinary powers. As much as I wanted to stay in bed, I pulled the blanket off me and got up. I looked back at Arty and smiled.

"If you like his thick black hair and protective blue eyes, you marry him."

"I've already got my man."

"Just my luck," I muttered and proceeded to get dressed. I went down on my knees to get my crossbow from under the bed.

"Are you going to catch a rabbit?"

"I am. Mama wasn't kidding. We could do with some rabbit for dinner."

Despite her name, Arty was not a hunter; she hated everything about it, and that included skinning and cleaning the rabbits we caught. "You're not going to make Markos a happy wife if you don't make his favorite food."

"Does that mean you know what his favorite meal is?"

"Arty, my darling cousin, your boy just got around to talking to me without hiding from me. I don't know what his favorite meal is, but I can accurately mimic him..." I exaggerated a surly look and doffed my imaginary hat. Arty fell back onto her pillow and laughed.

"You have to learn how to skin a rabbit for Markos, and I'll teach you how when I get back." I chuckled and left the room to peals of laughter that followed me down the corridor and out of the house.

CHAPTER 2

The bakery was a pleasant long walk away from the house, and I usually enjoyed the trail, but this wasn't one of those days. At least the rain had been replaced by a misty drizzle. That didn't improve my mood at all, nor did the puddles that I managed to stomp through.

There was another reason I wasn't looking forward to my early morning trip to the bakery. The baker's wife was going to indulge in one of her favorite pastimes. Kiria Despina was the local matchmaker, as well as being the baker's wife. She was a lovely woman except for the fact that she wanted to introduce me to boys that were 'good marriage material.' She needed a new pastime. Matchmaking in the village was a respected position, and Kiria Despina had a good track record. I wasn't sure what that meant, but my mother talked about her like she was the Saint of Matchmaking.

I trudged up the road towards the bakery in silence, which was surprising. It was far too quiet. I looked up into the trees and stopped. Birds usually nested at this time of the year, and it was usual to hear the cacophony of chirping birds when I made the journey to the bakery.

Not today. There was an eerie silence.

I slowly turned when I finally heard a bird's tweet... It was flying high in the sky surrounded by other birds, and it seemed they were abandoning their nests. Why was this bothering me? Chickens not laying eggs and birds flying away... It was at that moment that I remembered something my father once said about birds that sent a chill through me. Papa was talking about the 1928 Corinth earthquake and said that animals started to behave abnormally before the quake struck the city.

He said animals have a unique sense of things that we humans don't possess. Papa was in Corinth then, and it was an experience he never forgot. Something was going to happen, and soon if the birds and the chickens were an indication. I secured the crossbow across my back and set off down the road at full pelt.

I had rounded the corner leading to the church when I felt the low rumble under my feet.

Earthquake.

My father *was* right! It was the first time I felt the earth move under my feet, and it was the most unnerving thing I had experienced in my short life. I lost my footing and stumbled near the church steps. With my heart beating louder than the screams of the people who were streaming out of their houses, I got back up on my feet and almost fell over again. To my horror, when I looked up at the church landing, I saw my aunt Theodora on her knees. She was a nun and lived on the island of Patmos in the Holy

Annunciation Monastery. She rarely ventured back home, but she had made the journey for the christening.

"Aunty!" I screamed, but she couldn't hear me from the noise. My heart was in my mouth because if she didn't move, the loose blocks from the building were going to come down on her. I took to the stairs as if the dogs of hell had been unleashed and were after me. I reached the landing and tried to get Dora back on her feet. She looked at me, and it was then I saw the left side of her face covered in blood. "We have to move, Aunty!" I didn't wait for a reply. I helped her up, and we managed to get down the stairs. Just as we reached the bottom, the sound of the earth tearing itself apart made me shudder. I looked back at the church, and the loose blocks had come down on the landing just as I had feared.

I helped Aunt Dora sit on the ground while I used the small knife I had in my quiver and tore a strip of fabric off her long skirt. I used that to apply pressure to her bleeding head.

"We're in an earthquake!"

"I know, Zoe, I know. You must get to safety…"

"No, I can't leave you alone."

"My darling, go home and get out of the street. Our Lord will protect me."

I didn't give voice to the thought that God wasn't doing anything to protect anyone right now. "I need to get you to the hospital…"

"Zoe!" I looked up to find our village priest, Father Panayiotis Haralambos, running towards me, his crucifix violently swaying as he ran. He stopped and fell to his knees in front of us. "Sister Theodora!"

"Aunty is hurt, Father H. We need to get her to the hospital."

"We will, child, we will." With that, Father Haralambos signaled to one of the boys that had been following him. "Bless you, my child, bless you! We have much to do!"

Father Haralambos cupped my face and kissed the top of my head. He dusted himself off and pulled me up. We looked around at the devastation that surrounded us. All the homes near the church had either collapsed or were on fire. While he was giving orders to the boys, I turned back to my aunt.

"Father H will help you."

"Go help the family… you must help the family."

I kissed my aunt and set off on a dead run towards my family. My body was aching all over, and I found myself trying to avoid the debris of bricks and broken timbers. I couldn't stop because I feared what I would discover if I didn't run fast enough. There was pandemonium on the streets as I tried to go around people and debris. The cries of those trapped inside the houses will haunt me till the day I die. There was nothing I could do but run.

I wanted to run faster, but my body betrayed me. I had to stop and catch my breath because my lungs felt like they were on fire. I didn't want to sit down because if I did, I thought I wouldn't get up. My hands were hurting, and it was only then I realized I had gravel embedded in the palms of my hands, and my knees were bleeding. With whatever reserves God had given me, I set off again and rounded the bend into the street where Uncle Petros lived.

The chaotic scenes that I had witnessed on my way to them were even worse. The dust was making my eyes sting, and I felt my throat constrict. I could taste the grime in the back of my throat. I found a water-filled drum that hadn't fallen over and scooped some water to splash it on my face. I cupped the water and took a drink. I ran towards the house and saw the men were trying to take people out of the demolished building. I spotted my father and Uncle Petros, who were helping pull people out of his house. I was horrified to see it had utterly collapsed; had I not been sent to the bakery, I would have ended up in that pile of rubble. Mama, Arty, and my grandmother were in there!

"Papa!" I screamed and joined him just as Uncle Petros pulled away from a large block of cement and reached into the rubble. I couldn't see what he had found because my father blocked my view. Strong arms held me, and I realized that my cousin Stavros was trying to pull me away from the collapsed house. He picked me up and hauled me off like a sack of potatoes over his shoulder.

Naturally, I fought him because I was not a child, but he wouldn't let up and took me to the other side of the street. Miraculously, the houses on that side were still standing and unharmed.

The house belonged to Uncle Ignatius. Stavros unceremoniously dumped me on the floor, where I landed with a thump. I was sore, angry, and ready to scratch his eyes out. Stavros didn't say a word; he just left and shut the door.

I was going to bolt for the door when I felt arms around me, and I looked up to find my mother's tear-streaked face. "Mama!"

"God was protecting you, my child!" My mother

hugged the stuffing out of me. "We have a lot of work to do."

"Is everyone all right? I saw the house at..." I stopped talking when the door opened, and Arty walked through. She was covered in dust, and blood was on her hands, on her face and clothes. The anger that coursed through my body evaporated when I took Arty into my arms and held her.

"She's dead, Zoe."

"Who is dead?"

Arty turned towards me, her pain-filled eyes glistening with tears. "Yiayia Maria!"

CHAPTER 3

MARCH 02, 1941

MIDNIGHT

I stumbled to the back of Uncle Ignatius's back yard and slid down the base of the tree. It had stopped raining at some point in that God-forsaken day, but the ground was pot marked with holes where the rain had turned the soil into sludge. I flopped down onto the ground and found myself sitting in a puddle. I didn't care if I was sitting down in the cold mud, nor did I care that my stomach was growling, and I couldn't remember if I had eaten anything since that morning.

My beloved grandmother Maria had been killed. I couldn't believe it. At midnight she was making me laugh with her impressions of her crazy parrot and then...she was dead. I was numb and so tired that I could hardly keep my eyes open. The soles of my feet hurt even when I was sitting down. I contemplated the idea of just curling up and going to sleep in the mud. I drew a breath, and the cold air seared my nostrils. I wished this was a crazy dream caused by too much wine.

I looked down at the badly damaged birdcage in my hands. I had found it half-hidden in the rubble. I had this overwhelming feeling of guilt wash over me when I saw Polyxeni's broken body in the cage. I had killed her. She wanted out, and I didn't let her; she knew what was coming and wanted to escape. I managed to pry apart the bottom of the cage. I took out the battered body and held her. I was crying for a bird. I had cried so much during the day I thought I had no more tears left.

I glanced up when I heard the back door open. A lantern lit up my mama's weary face as she approached me. She looked as shattered as I felt. I could see the sheen of unshed tears in her green eyes, and her usually curly red hair that she always wore in a bun was cascading down her shoulders in dirty red ringlets. She was the most beautiful woman in the world, even when she was dirty. I wanted her to hold me. I wanted her to tell me that everything was going to be all right, that this was indeed a nightmare and I had just woken up.

Without saying a word, Mama put the lantern down, took Polyxeni from my hands, and sat down next to me. Right there in the puddle with me. She put her arm around me, and the floodgates opened. I felt like a child and I couldn't stop crying.

"Tell me everything will be all right."

Mama didn't say a word for a long time. "I can't."

"You can lie to me, Mama. I don't mind."

I felt her body shake with laughter and looked up to see

tears streaking down her face even though she was laughing. She kissed the top of my head and brushed her tears with the back of her hand.

"With God's help..."

"Dora!" I had just remembered my aunt.

"Dora is fine, and she's with her sisters tending to those who are hurt."

"Oh, good," I mumbled and settled in my mother's embrace. "I'm tired. Even my toes hurt..."

"I'm so proud of you, Zoe. You had worked hard throughout the day and night, even when you were tired."

"You look tired too."

My mother didn't respond; she tried, but every time she went to speak, her voice broke, and I could see the effort it was taking for her to even look at me. "I will be fine. With God's help, I will be."

"I got Polyxeni killed."

"No, you didn't. Polyxeni would have died in the earthquake anyway. She couldn't fly even if you let her out."

I glanced at the dead bird that lay in the mud for a long moment. "Do birds go to heaven?"

"I don't know, but if they do, your grandmother and Polyxeni are together."

I looked up at Mama. "Pappou will be there."

She didn't say anything for a moment. "They are together again."

"I wonder if he will fling his slippers at Polyxeni like he used to?"

My mother chuckled and wiped her eyes with the back of her sleeve. "Zoe, you brighten the darkest day."

I deepened my voice and gave the best impression of my grandfather that I could muster. "Maria! I'm going to roast that parrot!" My mother was laughing and crying at the same time. I was glad I made her laugh. My impressions of my grandfather always made my grandmother smile too. Now they were laughing together, up there somewhere.

A drizzle began to fall, and my toes had gone numb from the cold. In addition to my grandmother, we had lost quite a few of our family throughout the day. The wailing always signaled someone had lost their life. While I loved my cousins and the rest of the family, my favorite was my grandmother.

"We are going through the darkness, my darling. I want you to take Arty and go to Michael's house…"

I violently shook my head. "No."

"Not tonight, Zoe; don't disobey me."

"I'm not leaving you…"

"I love you very much, but you have to go. There will be–"

"No. I want to help you prepare…"

"That's not your job, my darling. That is the job of the older women of the family."

"What am I going to do while you are helping…" Helping to prepare the dead for burial is what I wanted to say, but I didn't.

"You are helping me. I know you will be safe at Michael's home, and before you say anything, Stavros has assured me it wasn't damaged."

"But–"

"Please. Listen to me. There are times we must do what

we don't want to do, but, in those times, we must remain steadfast, and we do it."

I wanted to protest.

I wanted to haggle with her, to make her understand that I was not a child, that I wanted to help. I didn't.

She was right despite my objections. "Can I say goodbye to Yiayia before I go to sleep?"

"Of course you can but..."

"I will be strong, Mama. Just like Yiayia said that Laskarina Bouboulina was strong."

"Your grandmother loved that woman." My mother's voice was breaking with emotion. "She was thrilled you had fallen in love with her heroine. You two are so much alike. She said that the boy who marries you would be the luckiest man alive. Only yesterday, your grandmother said she wanted to sing and dance at your wedding..." She took a deep breath. "You can say goodbye to her, and then you will take Arty and go to Michael's home, all right? Do you give me your word that you will do that?"

"Yes, Mama." I nodded. My word was good enough for her because in our family, if you swore an oath, it meant you made a covenant with God. My mother got up from the muddy puddle we were sitting in and gathered me into her arms. "God is on our side, my precious child. God is always on our side."

"He must have taken the day off..."

I was expecting a scolding for chastising God, but my mother shook her head and put her arm around my shoulders. She kissed me, and we walked back, caked with mud, through the rain, and to the house.

CHAPTER 4

MARCH 02, 1941

3 AM

God was playing a cruel trick on me. I was so tired, but I couldn't sleep for more than a couple of hours. After Arty and I left the house to go to Michael's home, we walked through the damaged town in disbelief. The streets were filled with people who didn't want to go back to their homes, or they had no homes. They slept out in the open away from covered areas in case loose building material would collapse on top of them.

"Arty, I can't feel my feet."

Arty stopped and looked down at my mud-splattered shoes. "They're still there."

I was about to respond when I heard trucks coming towards us. We watched them pass us. "Our soldiers have arrived."

Greek soldiers got out of a truck that stopped across the

road from my brother's house. It was followed by a second truck with more soldiers and supplies. To my surprise, we saw familiar faces: Arty's Markos, and the Athenian, Apostolos Kyriakou.

Arty started to giggle and nudged me when Apostolos caught sight of us and alerted Markos. They broke away from the group and joined us. Arty and Markos drifted to the side to have a private conversation while I was alone with Apostolos, who offered his condolences.

"Thank you." I wasn't sure what to say other than that.

"We're here to help."

"Can you bring back all those who have died?" As soon as I said it, I knew it was wrong. Apostolos was not to blame for the dead, nor was he to blame for the earthquake, but somehow, at that moment, he became my focus to vent my sorrow and fury.

To his credit, Apostolos shook his head. "If I were God, I could bring them back, but I'm not."

"It's too bad you are not. Who are those soldiers? They don't look like ours."

"English soldiers. They are sending more supplies, and they're going to help us."

I didn't have a chance to say anything else because both men were called away to rejoin their squad. The English had arrived to help us, and for the first time that day, I felt that we had not been forgotten. The English set up camp across the street from Michael's house. I lingered in the doorway and watched them unload supplies. After multiple tugs on my shirt, Arty pulled me inside.

The downstairs bedrooms stored all the furniture and assorted boxes. I had forgotten that Michael's house was in the process of being painted to get it ready for when he returned from the Albanian front. "I think we're going to sleep in the kitchen. Let's get some blankets and the flokati rugs so we won't have to sleep on the wooden floor. The last thing I want is splinters stuck in my butt."

"What if…"

"There won't be another earthquake, Arty. The big one has hit us."

"Are you sure?"

"That's what my mother said. Now, up you get before I decide to sleep on the steps."

"I'll push you up." It was a joke, but I wished she could push me up the stairs. I didn't want to trudge mud up there, so I took off my shoes and socks and left them by the door. My legs felt like they were made of lead, but we eventually went up the steps.

White sheets covered the wooden floors to protect them from any spilled paint, and empty paint drums served as chairs. We didn't care. I moved the paint drums away from us and set up our bed. We collapsed onto our rugs, and the moment our heads touched our pillows, our shattered world disappeared.

When I awoke, light from the street flooded the kitchen, but it wasn't morning. I checked my watch, and to my dismay, it was only three in the morning! I attempted to go back to sleep, but once I was awake, all hope for falling back asleep evaporated.

I kicked off the blanket and got to my feet. If I couldn't sleep, then I would get up; there was no point in looking up at the ceiling. I managed to accidentally kick a paint bucket and step on every creaky step going downstairs. Arty was usually a light sleeper, but tiredness won this time. I opened the front door and stood at the threshold. Despite the hour, there was a lot of movement of soldiers and Greeks. I felt my body shudder even though there was no cold wind to make me shiver. What do they say when this happens? Was someone stepping on my future grave? Something like that... I banished that thought from my mind. I didn't need to be reminded about death today. The rain had stopped, and the crescent moon was high up in the sky, casting its shadow across the once leafy street.

I was about to close the door when the air sirens sounded, sending everyone into a panic. My first mistake was to turn and bolt up the stairs leaving the door open. The screams coming from outside were matched by Arty calling my name from upstairs. Moments later, she came running down the stairs, pushed past me, and flew out the door.

I almost fell but managed to hang on to the railing, which broke my descent. As soon as I got out of the house, the broken shards of rock pierced my bare feet. I cursed myself for my stupidity while I quickly grabbed my shoes. The mud had stiffened the soft leather, but with some effort and a lot of cursing, I managed to put them on and set off after Arty like a woman possessed.

I had almost got to her when I heard the warplanes above me. I froze and just stared up as if the power to move had been taken away from me. I needed to run, but I couldn't move. I was frozen in place and ripe for a bomb to explode and end my short life.

That's when the bombs started dropping; one exploded further down the street, and I willed myself to run as fast as

I could to get to Arty. Everyone was trying to hide from the bombs, but there was no escape. Where were they going to land, and who was going to die? It was a game of roulette and the winner's prize was death.

Everyone was running away from the center of town, but I went the opposite way and ran after Arty, who was getting further away from me.

"Arty!" I screamed, but it was in vain. My voice was drowned out by the cacophony of sirens, screams, planes, and bombs. Above all the other noises, it was the whistling of the bombs before they exploded what pierced through the chaos that surrounded me.

To my horror, my beloved cousin kept running. The bombs seemed to be everywhere, and I frantically looked around for somewhere to hide.

There was no protection, so I chose to run faster than I could imagine, fueled by fear and determined to catch Arty before we both got killed. I stumbled over debris from the earthquake and lost my footing. I was angry with myself that I wasn't watching where I was going. That anger coursed through my body and powered me back up. I set off once again, rounded a corner, and found myself slamming into an English soldier. He didn't say a word but instead picked me up and hauled me out of the street as the bombing continued. When he put me back down, I could see he was not much older than me.

"Don't go out there! Stay here!" He spoke Greek with a heavy accent. I wanted to yell at him for wanting to hide, but I didn't have time to deal with a scared soldier. I tore myself away from him and bolted after Arty.

"Artemis Mavrakis! Stop! Dammit!" I screamed once

again, hoping she could hear me. I saw her look back at me for a moment. In that split second, when I thought she heard me and was about to run back to me, that infernal whistling sound echoed all around me. What I feared the most happened before me—a bomb hit the ground just meters from where Arty was standing. I watched in stunned disbelief as she was engulfed in flames from the explosion.

I fell to my knees while my world collapsed around me.

CHAPTER 5

APRIL 02, 1941

FARSALA

If someone had told me that I would willingly spend time in a cellar during the day and not want to go outside, I'd have thought they had lost their mind. Nearly all of my time was outdoors, and I did everything possible not to be inside unless it was dark or I was helping my mother in the house.

The days after the earthquake and bombings, it was like I wasn't in control of my mind or body. I felt that everything I did was pointless. What use was I to anyone when I couldn't save my best friend? All I had to do was close the door. If I had closed the door, Arty would not have gone past me and to her death. If only I had closed the door.

I could have stopped her.

I should have stopped her.

I was bigger and quicker than her.

If I had stayed in bed, I could have prevented her from running until we both left the house together and found shelter from the bombs.

I didn't.

I couldn't.

I had blood on my hands, and no amount of soap and water would ever get rid of it. I couldn't bring myself to find joy in anything I did. Mama said that no one blamed me for Arty's death. The Italians were to blame. She was wrong. There was someone that blamed me for her death.

I blamed myself.

It was something that would haunt me for the rest of my days, and since I am cursed with a photographic memory, erasing the look on her face moments before she died would be impossible to forget.

Over the following hours and days, the earth continued to rumble under our feet, and the Italian planes continued their bombings over our ruined city. We were at war. We were up against demons rather than human beings. How do you defeat demons?

I understand an earthquake destroying so many lives because that was just the natural order of the world, but I could never understand the barbarous Italians. Who bombs a shattered and homeless people after an earthquake? I will never understand their viciousness. They couldn't beat our mighty soldiers in Albania, so they decided to kill innocent people—my family, my friends, my countrymen.

Uncle Petros, Stavros, and two of my aunts, Evgenia and Antonia, came to live with us because their homes were in ruins. Our other family spread out and away from Larissa. The earthquake had spared our farm; the barn had a few bales of hay topple, and that was the extent of the damage.

The once private oasis that was my bedroom was no longer my own because my two aunts were sleeping there. I wanted to sleep in the barn, but Papa cleared out the cellar, and that was now my room.

It was a surprise to me because I had been banned from going down there ever since that time I went hunting with my brothers and came home with my catch of wild rabbits. Mama had skinned them, and they were salted and ready to pack up for winter. I went to the cellar, and when I opened the door, a rat scurried across and down the steps. I screamed, not because I'm afraid of rats, but because the little monster was huge and almost sent me headfirst down the stairs.

Unfortunately, in my exuberance to kill the rat, I fired my crossbow into the semi-darkness. I shot several arrows and let out a triumphant yell thinking I had killed the rat, but instead, I had shattered several of my mother's pickled vegetables and destroyed a few bottles of Papa's homemade brew. After that, I wasn't allowed in the cellar anymore.

Yet here I was. Me, the rats, and the pickled vegetables.

I could hear our visitors upstairs. I wondered when they were going to leave. I didn't want to see or talk to anyone; I wasn't in the mood for making mindless small talk or hear them say how sorry they were for our family's loss. I couldn't bear to listen to any of it. I lay back onto my makeshift bed and looked up at the wooden beams that were my ceiling. There were a couple of arrows stuck in the rafters that I would have to take down before Mama saw them. I didn't want to sketch or read. Nothing interested me.

The door to the cellar creaked. I ignored it. I knew who was coming down the steps long before they arrived–the gentle footfalls belonged to my mother.

"Zoe."

I turned my head and looked at my mother, who was standing just above the last step. She looked tired, but, unlike me, she couldn't run and hide.

"What did I say about going down to the river?"

"You said I should go down to the river." I could see her frustration with me etched on her face.

"Why haven't you done what I asked you to do?"

There weren't any windows in the cellar, and I couldn't use the 'I've got a headache' excuse that I had used the previous day.

"Because it's raining?"

I was expecting her to be upset at my surliness, but instead, she surprised me. She laughed. I know it was a genuine laugh because Mama always had one hand cradling her forehead while she laughed. It was as if she thought her head would fall off if she didn't keep it secure. I smiled because it had been a while since I had heard her laugh.

"Come here, child."

I got up from my bed and sat down on the stairs next to her. She put her arm around me and kissed the top of my head.

"It's a beautiful day, and I want you to go outside. I want you to draw me a beautiful portrait of you and your brothers."

I was confused. Mama had a photographic memory; that's who I inherited that special gift from. She didn't need another portrait.

"I want you to enjoy your childhood, my darling. You've been holed up down here and have done nothing but eat and sleep. You can't continue to live this way."

"I don't want to enjoy myself when I know Arty and Yiayia Maria are dead."

"You've spent enough time thinking about what you could have done differently. You've spent far too much time on the 'what if…'"

"I could have saved Arty."

My mother sighed. "My darling girl, sometimes we can't protect those we love. You can't stop living because they are no longer with us, and we can't wallow in our pain for the rest of our lives."

"I mourn them; that's not wallowing in pain."

"You are hurting. You want to lash out and scream at everyone. There is something you have to remember. If you allow bitterness to grow in your heart, that's all that will be there. You are not to blame for Arty's death. Remember our five-minute wallow rule?"

"Yes. We can wallow for five minutes, and then we get up to confront it or to resolve our dispute. But there is nothing to resolve. They're gone, and God won't bring them back."

"The dead are not resurrected here on earth, my darling. They are in heaven." Mama put her arms around me and I felt her strength as she held me. I didn't want her to let go of me. "If Arty were here now, would she want you to be like this?"

"No, but–"

She put her fingers lightly against my lips. "Today, we are free to go wherever we want. Tomorrow we may have that freedom taken away. You must live every day as if it were your last day of freedom."

I stared up at my mother and listened to what she was saying. Grief and loss had wrapped themselves around my heart, and I felt this overwhelming need to cry.

"You can't let sorrow or fear consume you."

"They don't consume me." My voice wavered. "I don't want to go down to the river."

"Even if it was a favor to me?"

I leaned into my mother and sighed. "Of course, I would do anything for you."

"Even going down to the river?"

My mother knew just the right thing to say and how to get me to do as she asked.

"I know you don't want to go, but I want a new painting from you so I can add it to our family wall."

"How many black clouds do you want?"

"I'm certain there won't be any black clouds. We have to live for today, Zoe. Not for what might have been or was. Will you go down to the river for me?"

"Yes, Mama."

"That's my girl." Mama kissed my cheek and smiled. "We are going to have some guests for dinner, and they come from a country that is very far from us. I think you will enjoy listening to their stories."

I protested loudly. "You want me to go to the river *and* entertain people from another country?"

"Yes. It's not hard, and you might enjoy meeting them."

"What country are they from?"

"Australia."

"If I must."

"That's my girl. Come home before the sun sets so you can help me set the table."

CHAPTER 6

I wasn't in the mood to sketch, but I had promised my mother I'd go to the river. That's what I was doing, even if it was to watch the water flow downstream. A promise is a promise. The depressing weather that matched my mood had given way to a beautiful, warmish Spring day.

I rode my bicycle down the dusty road while being distracted by the increased presence of foreign soldiers. I had wallowed in my sorrow for too long and failed to notice what was going on around me. Not paying attention was surely going to get me killed.

A truck's horn blared behind me, causing me to lose my balance on the bike. I struggled to stay upright, and I almost got it under control until I veered off the road and onto the gravel. That was the end of my valiant attempt to salvage my pride.

I would have told the driver what I thought of him, but by the time I looked up from the mess I had made of myself, the truck had disappeared. My bicycle's front wheel had hit a tree trunk, and three of the spokes had broken, and my dress looked like I had been rolling around in the dirt.

So much for a beautiful day sketching outdoors. But I had given my word to Mama... I decided to leave my damaged bike and walk to the river. A promise is a promise.

I slung my satchel over my shoulder and walked down the road. Things were changing rapidly, and the life I had known before the earthquake was almost a distant memory–tents and soldiers had replaced fields that used to be teaming with workers collecting the harvest.

"Zoe!"

I looked around to see someone was waving at me. At first, I wasn't sure who it was because the soldier was wearing a hat, and his face was obscured by a box he was holding. It was only when he put the box down that I recognized him.

Arty was right about her boy. He did have a beautiful smile. His eyes, black as tar, lit up and let his smile shine through.

"What happened to you? Where is Aphrodite?" Markos said as he approached me. He always looked a little awkward and shy whenever he spoke to me, but I was impressed that he remembered the name of my bicycle. I didn't think he had paid any attention to what I was doing because he only had eyes for Arty. I was wrong.

"Well, add a truck and some gravel, and you get a broken Aphrodite. I lost the battle."

"Are you hurt?"

"Oh, no, I'm fine." I tapped the hat on his head. "What is that?"

"It's called a hat, and you put it on your head."

I laughed for the first time since the earthquake and Arty's death. For a brief moment, I didn't feel guilty that I was alive, and my best friend wasn't. We looked at each other and smiled as we shared this moment of temporary joy.

"Why are you wearing that strange hat?"

Markos took it off and showed me the side of the broad brim was upturned in an odd fashion. If the cap was supposed to be a protection from the sun, it wasn't designed properly. "It's called a 'slouch' hat."

"I call it a 'stupid' hat because it doesn't protect you from the sun."

Markos chuckled and put the hat on my head. "It suits you."

It was far too big for my small head, even with the scarf that I was wearing. I must have looked silly. I laughed anyway because it *was* ridiculous. I placed the hat over Markos's dark hair and smiled.

"The Australian soldiers wear them. That's who I'm helping over there." He pointed to a larger group of soldiers that were setting up their tents. "The boys and I are helping the Australians set up camp here, and then we are heading out."

"Where are you going?"

"I don't know. All I know is we are leaving tonight."

"You're not old enough to join the army."

Markos didn't look like he took offense at what I had said, which was true. He was only sixteen years old, and I knew men had to be older than that to be fighting.

"We are all soldiers now. Everyone must defend our homeland."

"We are winning in Albania, so the war is nearly over." Markos frowned and didn't look convinced. I wasn't confident that was true either, but I clung on to that hope, or was it a lie?

"The Germans are coming, little cousin."

"We don't know that."

"That's why the Allies are here–the English, Australians, and New Zealanders. They are all here to protect us."

"We will beat the Germans as we did the Italians. We will fight and win."

"For the glory of Greece." Markos turned back and motioned to some of the other soldiers. He turned back to me. "I have to get back. If I don't see you before I leave, I will keep you in my prayers."

"I know you hunt, but can you shoot straight?"

I don't think Markos was expecting that question. A smile creased his face, and he nodded. "I can."

I was at a loss for what to say next. I was wearing two gold crosses; one was mine, and the other had belonged to Arty. I hadn't planned to give it to Markos, but I knew that Arty would have wanted me to do so. I took off the chain from around my neck and removed my crucifix. I motioned for Markos to lean down and I placed the chain with Arty's cross around his neck and kissed him on the cheek.

"No, Zoe. I don't want to take that away from you."

"Arty would have wanted you to have it. She loved you, and I think you loved her. You will fight for the glory of

Greece and in remembrance of her. I want you to have it and know that she is with you."

Markos cleared his throat and nodded. He placed his hand over the crucifix.

We stood there awkwardly, and then I tapped him on the arm. "Go, before those boys over there lose their arms. They are waving them so much they might take flight!"

Markos chuckled and kissed me on the cheek, and then he walked away and joined his fellow soldiers.

I shuddered as a cold blast of wind gave me goosebumps. The weather had changed in the time I had been talking to Markos. The wind had picked up and the air had a hint of impending rain. The sky had turned a deep purple and dark clouds hovered in the distance. The weather mirrored our fate.

CHAPTER 7

APRIL 10, 1941

FARSALA

I couldn't believe it had been just over a month since my world collapsed. It felt like everything was moving so fast — happy one day, and destruction and death the next. I didn't think my life would change again so quickly, but then I should have known not to tempt the Fates.

Earlier that morning, my cousin Stavros and I headed for the southern field. We had jars of pickled vegetables, and our precious cargo needed to be stored in an underground cellar. We were preparing for war.

After my chores were done, I wanted to go down to the river to draw, and Mama had told me that I could take some time to enjoy the day after I finished.

I had spent weeks not being able to draw, but I found that it once again brought me joy to see my cousin's face appear in my sketchbook. I had so much art to show my brothers when they returned from the front lines. My brothers were big, strong men, and I loved them dearly, but they could be annoying. It didn't matter. I missed them and wanted them home.

They gave me their word that they were coming home. I had clung to that promise since I watched all three walk away from the farm. I had overheard that news about the war and our men had reached Larissa. I had to go home and find out when my brothers were going to return. Maybe they were already back while I was busy by the river.

I raced the storm clouds in joyous anticipation of running into my brothers on the road leading to our home. I was going so fast that I almost ended up rolling my bicycle into a ditch. Luckily, I managed to stay upright. I reached the farmhouse and skidded to a stop just in time to see Father Haralambos enter the house.

Father H was here? What did he want? Maybe he was here for dinner with the Australian soldiers. It had been a while since we had a big feast. I left the bike on the ground and picked up my bag.

When I went inside, I knew it was terrible news that had brought the priest to our home. There was no laughter and it felt like joy had been sucked out of the entire house. I saw my papa first. He wore his best coat, which he only wore on Sundays to go to church. And he wasn't wearing it as he usually did, but it was draped over his shoulders instead as if it was a cloak. That was never a good sign. Papa only wore it on his shoulders when someone in the family died.

At first, I thought it was my great-aunt Evgenia. She was over a hundred, and if anyone were going to die, she would be the one. However, she wasn't dead because she was wailing in the corner. I hadn't seen her because my attention was focused on my father.

Mama was crying and hanging on to Papa. My father was a tall, sturdy man, but he looked so tiny as he hung on to Mama. I had never seen my father cry before and it unnerved me. I didn't want to ask who had died.

Father Haralambos saw me and got up to greet me. He was wearing his black flowing robes and that giant crucifix around his neck. His blue eyes looked into mine, and I could see the sorrow. Papa came to me. He took my hand and led me to the sofa, where I sat down between him and Mama.

"We have some terrible news…"

"Who died?" I asked and reached out to touch his cheek. Tears filled his eyes, and even his upturned mustache looked to be drooping. "Whoever died is now with God, Papa."

"My darling child. God has called your brothers home…"

No. That wasn't right. No. I didn't believe it. God had promised that my brothers were going to come home. That's what Father H had said. God PROMISED that he would keep the Greeks safe. My brothers *promised* they were going to come back from the war.

A promise is a promise.

Little did I know then that God breaks many promises.

I didn't think my heart could shatter into any more pieces, but it did. The pain consumed me, and there was nothing I could do or say. How could this be? Were my brothers really dead? No, there had to be some mistake.

There was no mistake.

My brothers were never coming back, just like my beloved Arty and my grandmother Maria. Gone. Just like that.

Taken by God.

I hated God.

CHAPTER 8

APRIL 16, 1941

FARSALA

They were here. The cannons were so loud that I initially thought it was thunder, but I could hardly see the stars through the window in the loft where I had been sitting since the battle started raging. The stars had virtually disappeared behind the smoke. The war had finally arrived, and I could hear the cannon shells exploding in the hills– loud explosions of bombs tearing at the cliffs and at our boys, who were engaging them. We all knew this day would come. The talk of the village was about *when* the Germans would get to us.

Now we were fighting the Germans in our country. They had invaded my home and killed my family. They bombed us every night, and although we were in Farsala and not in Larissa, their bombs reached us as well. People were trying to escape, but it was a futile effort to hold death at bay; death always won. Night after night, the bombs rained down upon us and bodies lay out in the fields. Papa thought I was too young to know the real horror of war, but I wasn't blind.

Our family scattered. Uncle Petros took my aunts into the mountains and away from the bombing, but he wasn't running away. He came back and was ready to fight the invaders. The last we heard from Ellie and Angelos, they were in Thessaloniki with Aunt Stella, but the Germans had captured the city and we didn't know if they were still alive.

I overheard Papa say that the enemy was at the gate, and everyone needed to be in the fight. He was right. The Australian and New Zealand soldiers were fighting for our freedom; their countries were on the other side of the world but here they were fighting for us. I had grown to like these men a great deal; they were brave and honorable.

Now there was no question about whether we were going to fight like our ancestors. It was time for war.

I had to get down from the loft because our horse, Zeus, was being spooked by the loud noises. I was scared as well, and I looked up into the heavens and closed my eyes. I had a complicated relationship with God. It was an opinion I kept to myself because every time I told whoever wanted to listen that I hated God, they would lecture me. No one wanted to hear what I thought about God.

I hated God, but today, I was ready to ask him for help. I prayed for victory and promised that if he helped us, I would do my chores without question, and I would do what was asked of me. I didn't expect an answer right away. Father Haralambos always said that God doesn't answer your prayers as soon as you ask him. I wondered if God knew how much I hated him on days when my pain of losing my brothers, Arty, and my grandmother coursed through my veins. He probably knew and didn't care.

"Loud night for you, Zeus," I said.

The horse shoved his head towards me, and I giggled at his playful nature. Zeus was a beautiful animal–a chestnut Arravani that had been born on our farm. We had quite a few horses, but Zeus was my favorite. I named all the animals on the farm, much to my brothers' amusement. Everyone needed a name, even animals.

"I'm sure that the Germans will be defeated, or at least I hope so because I just prayed to God and that doesn't happen very often. We beat the Turks in 1821, then the Italians. Now it is the Germans who will feel the full force of our brothers." Did I truly believe that?

I'm sure if Zeus could have talked, he would have questioned my belief in a God that I didn't trust but just prayed to while wishing that I was wrong about him. I would have asked Satan himself for help if it could help us win the war.

A loud explosion that lit up the dark sky made me jump as the noise reverberated through the night. "Oh, that must have destroyed several of those Germans tanks." I wasn't sure who I was trying to convince; maybe saying the words out loud made me believe them more. I'm sure Zeus didn't care.

"Zoe, come inside, child," Mama called out to me and soon joined me. I looked up to find her looking at me in sorrow. She had been crying again.

"It's all right, Mama. God is on our side. Listen to those

rockets. That's the Allies—they are winning, and we are beating those horrible Germans like we beat the Italians!"

My mama's gaze turned to the mountains, and she sighed. "God willing, we will all come out of this alive. I'm sure with you praying to Him, He will give us extra protection."

I wondered if she was teasing me. She looked as if she was trying not to laugh but lost that battle when she pulled me into her arms.

"God listens to your prayers even if your faith is as tiny as a mustard seed."

"I think it's smaller than that. Father H said we have God on our side and that means we will win and I'm going to believe Father H because–"

"Don't call the reverend 'Father H.'"

"Why?"

"It's not respectful. Father Haralambos is a man of God, and we should show him respect."

I didn't think it was disrespectful to call him Father H., "I don't think God is going to mind."

Despite her tears, my mother laughed. I had missed hearing that beautiful laugh. She kissed the top of my head. "You are going to give me a lot of grief as you grow older, but I love you."

"I love you too," I replied and wrapped my arms around her waist. "All that noise is scaring Zeus. I think I'm going to put him in the barn."

"Papa is going to hitch the wagon to Zeus, and we are going to Thieri's cabin."

"Now? Are we going to watch the battle from Athena's Bluff?"

"We're not watching any battle. Papa wants us to be safe up in the mountain. I want you to come inside and help pack."

"Why are we going to the cabin? Why aren't we staying here? Are we going to run while the battle rages?"

"We are not running. Papa wants us safe..."

"Papa is not running, is he?"

"No. Didn't I tell you why we are not staying here? It's not safe. Don't ask so many questions, child."

"If I don't ask questions, how will I learn anything? You keep telling me that I need to ask if I want to find out."

"We don't have a lot of time," Mama said and went back inside.

"I don't know why we are going to the cabin, but we will see the battle from there. Our boys will win the war against the Germans. I love Athena's Bluff, Zeus. We will have a perfect view of the Germans from up there."

Athena's Bluff was where my brother Thieri had built his home. It was a cabin fit for a king, he would say. The view from the outcrop was of Tempi Valley, and you could see Mount Ossa in the distance. One day I was going to see what was beyond Mount Ossa. I wanted to go to Athens and then travel the world. It would be so exciting to go to all the places I had read about.

I patted the horse one more time and walked back to the farmhouse. When I entered the living area, there were blankets piled high on chairs and on the sofa, and two suitcases sitting near the kitchen.

I navigated around the suitcases and entered the kitchen. The smell of bread permeated the room. Five loaves were cooling on the table, and another two were in the oven. Mama had taken out pickled vegetables stored in jars from the pantry. Before I had a chance to ask what was going on, she gave me a white bed sheet that had been ripped into long strips. "Take these to Papa and tell him I'll be ready in about thirty minutes."

I collected the makeshift bandages and quickly walked the short distance to my room. It felt strange to knock on my door, but I did and entered. Lying on my bed was an Australian soldier, Jimmy Peterson. His right trouser leg had been torn from the knee down, and a large bandage was wrapped around his lower leg. It didn't look healthy at all, and I doubt he would be able to stand on it.

My papa was the tallest of the men that were around the bed. When he saw me, his smile reached his eyes, and they crinkled in delight. Sitting next to him were Apostolos and another Australian soldier. They had been at the farm for the last three days trying to get their friend well enough to join their comrades. Sergeant Clarence spoke Greek but with a strange accent, which was funny.

Papa stood and took the bandages from me. "I'm so proud of you. You have been a big help to our guests, and God will reward you for your loving spirit. Don't be afraid."

"I'm not afraid. Our friends and our brothers will beat them back to where they came from, won't you, Sergeant Clarence?"

"We will win, little sister."

"God willing, we will be victorious," Papa said and kissed me on the cheek.

"Mama said she would be ready in thirty minutes."

"Good. Now I'm going to change the bandages. Why

don't you take Sergeant Clarence and help him load the wagon?"

"All right," I said and waited for the soldier to join me before we left the room. Sergeant Clarence greeted Mama before he picked up the blankets, and we headed outside. It didn't take us long to get the wagon ready.

"So, how is the picture coming along?" Sergeant Clarence asked me as he sat down on an upturned bucket near the barn.

"Drawing!" I corrected him and laughed at how he got the word wrong. "How did you learn Greek?"

"My grandmother is Greek."

"Where was your grandmother from?"

"Constantinople. When they threw them out, she went to Egypt."

"Is that why you have a funny accent?"

Sergeant Clarence laughed. "No. That's my Australian accent. My grandmother met my grandfather, who is an Australian, and they went to live there."

"Say something in Australian?"

Clarence gazed down at me and then smiled. "Bonzer sheila," he said. I didn't know what it meant, but he translated it. "You are an excellent young woman."

"Bonzer sheila," I repeated, and it made no sense to me, but I liked how it sounded.

"You should come to Australia, ZoZo."

I laughed when he called me by that nickname. He must have overheard Papa. "I want to see what's out there beyond Mount Ossa. After you defeat the bad men, I want to go to Athens and study art, like Mama, and then I'll come to Australia and see that bridge... oh," I said and then remembered I had something for him. I fished around in my pocket and brought out the photograph that Clarence had given me. I raced into the barn and came back with my sketchbook. Flipping through the pages, I found the artwork for the Sydney Harbour Bridge. "This is for you."

Clarence took it and smiled. "Wow, this is beautiful. Can I keep it?"

"Do you really like it? Yes, you can keep it."

"One day, you are going to be a great artist. I will take you to this bridge."

That's all we had time for because Papa and Apostolos came out of the house. They loaded supplies onto the wagon and put a blanket and hay to cushion the ride for the wounded soldier. It looked like Papa was going with them, and I didn't want him to leave. I felt like a coward; we were running to the mountains like scared rabbits. I was torn between wanting to face the enemy and being terrified of what was to come. So much for wanting to be just like my heroine, Laskarina Bouboulina.

"Are you going with them?"

My father took my hand and walked to a nearby chair where he sat down, and I sat on his lap. I felt safe with his strong arms around me. "I have to go with Apostolos and the boys around the gorge to evade the Germans," he said.

"Why can't Apostolos do it? I thought you were coming with us to the cabin."

"No, I'm going to join in the fight. We must stop the Germans. I want you and Mama to go to the cabin. Don't come down from the mountain until I come for you, all right?"

"You are coming back to get us, right?"

"I will come back once the fight is over."

"Alright, but why do you have to go?"

Papa hugged me tightly. "I know a secret way around the gorge. Do you remember the summer we went hunting and Theo caught that wild pig? That's where we are going."

I looked up at my father as the gunfire and exploding artillery sounded louder and closer. I could smell the gunpowder in the air and knew that we had to leave. "You will be back, right?"

"I will be back."

"You promise?" I asked and hoped he would utter the words I wanted to hear. I needed my father to say the words that would ease my rising fear. "A promise is a promise?"

"I can't promise. No one can promise..."

"But..."

"Zoe, we are going to try to stop the Germans, but you have to do your part. You have to be strong and be brave, just like Laskarina Bouboulina. Whatever happens, my little girl, you must be courageous and never let anything stop you."

"I'm running away to Athena's Bluff. That's not being brave."

My father didn't say anything for the longest time and just held me. "You are not a coward, little one. We are all scared, but we must fight."

"You will come back to us, Papa."

"God willing, I will come back."

I didn't want to think about what my father had just said. Of course, he was coming back. He couldn't leave us. "I don't want you to go."

"If I don't go, how are we going to win this war?

Remember the brave men and women during the Liberation? They had to go and fight for our country." Papa tipped my face towards him and gazed into my eyes. "Have I told you how much I love you?"

"Yes, this much." I threw back my arms. "I love you even bigger. Bigger than Mount Ossa!"

"Only that much?" Papa teased and then kissed me on the cheek. "Be brave, be strong, and listen to Mama until I come back. Can you do that for me?"

"Yes, Papa, but—"

"Shh." Papa wrapped his strong arms around me and kissed me on the head. "Be brave."

The brave fight, but cowards run. "Yes, I will be brave."

"I love you, and never forget how much. You are my favorite daughter."

"I'm your only daughter." I wanted to cry and beg him not to leave, but I couldn't. He was going to save the Australians and then fight for our freedom.

"That's why you're my favorite," Papa replied as he gently tapped his finger on my nose. "Now, I have to get up and say goodbye to your mama. It may be a few days before I come to the cabin to bring you back to the farm."

Papa walked away and went towards Mama, who was anxiously standing by the wagon. He put his arm around her waist, and even in the darkness, I could see how much they loved each other. I thought that if I ever got married, I wanted to be able to look at my husband the way my mama looked at my father. I knew I might never find one person to love like that, but if God was listening, that's what I wanted. I wanted God to win the war for us, to make me a great artist, and to help me find someone to love with all my heart. That wasn't too much to ask.

It was getting late, and we boarded the wagon. I desperately wanted to hang on to my father but knew he had a job to do. Papa led Zeus towards the road, and the other cart followed us until we got to the crossroads. Papa gave me another kiss on the cheek and kissed my mother on the lips before he walked back to the covered wagon.

I turned in my seat to see him get on board. He looked back at us as the wagon turned and made its way down the road.

"Come back to us, Papa," I cried out as Mama led Zeus towards Athena's Bluff.

CHAPTER 9

APRIL 18, 1941

ATHENA'S BLUFF

"Zoe! The last thing I need is for you to fall out of that tree!" My mother's voice rang out from the entrance of the cabin. She had been repeating this warning every hour. I suspected it gave her something to do other than worrying about my father.

The war was still raging in the valley, and I hoped the Allies were beating the Germans. I looked up into the cloudy sky and prayed to God; he was going to be faithful to his word. One scripture my mama liked to recite is Psalm chapter 55 and verse 22: 'Cast thy burden upon the Lord, and he shall sustain thee: he shall never suffer the righteous to be moved.' "Well, time to pay up, God, and show me. I'm casting my burden on you."

"Zoe! Get down from the tree!"

"I'm watching the war, and we're winning!"

"Come down from there!"

"No, I want to wait for Papa. It's not cold," I yelled down from my perch on the highest tree I could find to climb. It was cold, and the little cover the tree was giving me wasn't enough to stop the rain from pelting me in the face. I shivered because I was wearing a light sweater and it was soaked. I wasn't going to move until my father returned, or I fell out of the tree.

Other than it being useless protection from the weather, the tree afforded me the view of the path leading up the mountain. It also allowed me to see the battle, at least the part of the fight that wasn't covered by the trees. Explosion after explosion, gunfire echoed in the valley as the Allies battled the Germans.

Greece had held off tyrants before. Ms. Keratsis told us that in the gorge where the Germans were now raging like mad dogs, another country had tried to invade us. The King of Persia tried to beat Greece with his massive army, but we drove him back. I knew my history, and the Greeks are a mighty force. We were going to be victorious.

Since we had come to Athena's Bluff two nights before, we had my mother's sister, Polly, brought to the cabin by Stavros. I wasn't sure why she had been in the hospital. No one told me anything, but it was terrible enough for her to be in the hospital. She didn't look well. The hospital was evacuated, and German planes were always bombing Larissa. I saw them flying overhead, and they made an awful noise.

The sound they made reminded me of the night Arty was killed, and that made me want to hurl something at those demon planes. They came in so low that if I reached up, just a little, I would have been able to touch them. Of course, I couldn't, but if I had had a gun, I could have brought one of those airplanes down. They screeched overhead and dropped bombs into the valley, and Stavros told me Larissa was on fire. There was no escaping these demons. I saw the planes and wondered why our aircraft were not fighting them.

"Mama! I see someone coming up the pass!" I screamed out and berated myself that I had forgotten to take my telescope from the farm. I couldn't make out who it was. Hopefully, it wasn't a German, or else we would be in terrible trouble. I had also forgotten to take my crossbow. I was not prepared as a good soldier should have been. I wasn't going to make that same mistake again if I made it off the mountain alive.

I pulled back my wet hair out of my eyes and tried to focus on the path. I had no weapon, and I couldn't break the tree limb to use it because it was too thick. I was desperate to use something to defend Mama and Aunty Evgenia. I slapped myself on the head when I remembered that Papa stored the metal rods for the lamb spit we had on Easter in the woodshed. I scrambled down the tree, skinning my knee and shins on my way down. I was now cold, wet, and bleeding, but I didn't care. I had to get the metal rods before whoever was coming got here.

I could barely see anything. The torrential downpour stung my face like a thousand mosquitoes had descended on Athena's Bluff and found my face. I slipped and slid my way to the woodshed and collapsed in an undignified heap on the wet floor. I didn't want to move, but I had to because whoever was coming up the pass was going to be here soon. I hoped that the rain would stall them long enough for me to find the rods.

I mustered up the strength to get myself off the floor and find the rods behind the woodpile. They were a little heavy, but I could use both hands to wield them like a sword.

I threw open the door of the shed and raced out. The rain had not stopped, but at least I could see in front of me without thinking that I was losing my eyesight. I ran down the path, metal rod in hand, to meet the danger.

Stavros was wearily trudging up the now slippery, mud-soaked path. He used a broken limb to keep from slipping and tried to steady himself when I ran into him at full pelt. A tree limb was the only thing that stopped us from careening down the path. I fought off Stavros' hands as he tried to hold me in place; I wanted to see if my father was coming up the pass.

My father wasn't behind him. Stavros had promised that the next time I saw him, he would have my father with him.

"Where's Papa?"

Stavros did not answer me; he hung his head and didn't meet my eyes. His wet hair was a mass of black curls, and I wasn't sure if he was crying. There was no time to ask him anything because someone else was coming.

Papa was here! The rain had lessened, and the skies were also quiet from the demonic Stukas. I ran down the path and reached a slight bend. I whooped and hollered, thinking my father was around the corner.

It wasn't my father.

Coming up the path were Father Haralambos and Apostolos. I slipped in the mud and came to a stop only when Apostolos broke my descent. He helped me up as Father Haralambos braced himself against the tree. Undoubtedly, my father was just behind them.

"Where is Papa?" I asked and tried to see past the thick knot of trees and brush. "Is he bringing the wagon? We've been up here for days, and we don't know what's going on!"

"Let's get out of the rain first, my child, and then we–"

"No!" I put both hands on the cleric's black cassock and stopped him in his tracks. "Where is my father?"

"Zoe, it's raining. As you can see, it's not about to stop. Let us all get into the cabin so we can talk," Apostolos tried to reason with me.

"I want to know where my father is!"

"Your mother is waiting to hear as well. It's not fair to make her wait longer than necessary." Stavros tried to reason, but I ignored him. He did the only thing that appeared to come to mind. He picked me up and slung me over his shoulder. I was surprised and screamed in outrage as they trudged up the path. The only sounds were my yelling, the oncoming Stukas, and the howling wind.

* * *

I braced myself against the back of the door and watched my mother being comforted by Father H. I had heard the words, but I didn't want to believe them.

Papa was dead. No, it wasn't possible. Not my father. It couldn't be right. Maybe he was on his way, and Apostolos had lost track of him. My father was NOT dead. He couldn't be. Today was his birthday, and I had drawn his portrait. He was NOT dead.

"HOW DID YOU LOSE MY FATHER?" I yelled at Apostolos, who was looking at me with those sad blue eyes of his. Those eyes were looking more freakish than they usually did. He had unnaturally blue eyes, and I hated them.

"I didn't..."

"You left Papa out there and didn't go back to look for him?"

"Zoe! That's no way to speak to Apostolos!"

I never talked back to my mama, but this time, I just had to. "Apostolos left Papa out there, with the Germans!"

My mama was horrified. I could tell from the way she narrowed her green eyes and her brow furrowed. Usually, what followed was either her slipper would come flying and hit me on the legs, or I would be without my books and sketchbook. I preferred the sandal. I didn't care what happened now because it didn't matter. Nothing mattered anymore.

"Why are you still alive?" I yelled at Apostolos after listening to everything he said. It was a pack of lies. I pushed away from the door and came up to Apostolos, who stood more than a foot taller than me. He was broad-shouldered with black hair, and those light blue eyes made him seem demonic. I hated the way he was looking at me. I hated everything about him. I despised him so much that I spat in his face. He didn't move.

"Why aren't you dead? There's not a mark on you," I yelled at him and tried to find any sign that he was injured, but he looked undamaged and far too healthy.

"Zoe! What did I say?" My mother admonished me, but I took no note of her. Nor did I pay attention to my aunt, who was in the corner praying. Why was that woman praying? It was too late for that!

"Respect is earned, Mama. Apostolos is lying. Athenians lie all the time!"

"I am not lying." Apostolos almost dropped to his knees in what seemed to me to try to convince me he was telling the truth.

"The cart overturned and your father–"

I did not wait to hear the rest. I struck him with my open hand. Apostolos did not react, which only made me angrier. I ran to the door and slammed it shut right behind me.

I stood on the balcony. The rain had not subsided, but I didn't care anymore. I made my way to the unprotected bluff that overlooked Tempi Gorge in a rage. I trembled with anger at God for taking my father.

"I HATE YOU!" I yelled out and felt my heart crushed at the thought that my father was dead. He was gone.

"I HATE YOU, GOD! I HATE YOU! YOU PROMISED! A PROMISE IS A PROMISE!" I screamed and knew it was useless because God didn't care. I sank to my knees and wept for my papa and what was to become of all of us. God had abandoned and betrayed me.

CHAPTER 10

I took out my rage against God in the shed. I smashed the poker against the wall so many times I made several dents into the wooden beams, but I didn't care. I exhausted myself and slipped down the wall with nothing but anger flowing through my veins.

"Can I come in?"

I heard Father Haralambos's voice from outside the woodshed. I was angry with everyone, angry with the Germans, the Greeks, and God. I especially didn't want to see that Athenian coward because I would kill him for not saving my father. I didn't want to speak to the priest.

"Go away!" I yelled out. I hoped he had the good sense to listen to me and thought that he did, but there was another knock on the door.

"I'm not going away." Father Haralambos wasn't going to be deterred', no matter how many times I told him to leave me alone.

The wind was howling outside, and I could feel the cold

under my bare feet. Despite my anger at the priest, I couldn't let him stay out in the rain. I opened the door to find Father H soaked to the skin.

I beckoned him inside. If I hadn't been angry, I would have laughed—his robes were plastered to him, and his kalimavkion was also soaked, and the water had dripped down his face. I didn't laugh because my heart couldn't muster the energy to see anything other than darkness. He was just a man who was soaking wet. Father H took a seat on a pile of logs and waited.

"The tears of God are washing over our country, Zoe."

"Why is God crying? He's the one who broke his promise, and my papa is dead. You promised me that God was on our side."

"He *is* on our side."

"You're lying! The enemy isn't just at our door, Father. He's broken in! Is that being on our side? Papa died because he believed God was on our side!"

"Your papa still lives. He is in heaven with God..."

"I don't want him in heaven! I want him here with us. I don't want him to be with Michael, Thieri, and Theo! I want him HERE!" I screamed at Father H, who withstood my anger, and his demeanor never changed. Instead, he got up from the woodpile and came to sit next to me.

"Zoe..."

"You lied to me. I trusted you. I trusted God. You both betrayed me."

"I didn't lie to you. I said God was on our side, and He is. Do you remember all the lessons you have heard in church about striving for good and how God will reward you?"

"That's not going to happen now. It's all lies."

"Are you calling *me* a liar?"

"Yes," I replied angrily, knowing I had just accused an honest man of a crime he didn't commit. When I'm angry, I don't hold back, and my brain says stupid things.

"I know you don't mean that. I also know you don't truly believe that God killed your Papa."

"You don't lie, but you have to repeat what God says." I glanced at Father H, who was watching me.

"It's not a lie, Zoe. God is on our side. You have to believe that because we have to believe in hope. Our world is on fire, and the demons are walking the earth. Do you remember that God said that the devil would be walking about like a roaring lion? That's what he is doing now. When a wild beast is loose, people die."

"Why doesn't God kill the German and Italian pigs? Why doesn't he send a bolt of lightning and set them on fire? I would have done that."

"Our job, little one, is to resist the invaders like our forefathers did so many years ago. God will avenge the fallen, but we have to do our part."

"I'll take a gun and shoot them all."

"That's not your job. Your job, my child, is to help your mama through this difficult time. Then, after forty days, you can join the Resistance."

I hated waiting for anything, and now I had to wait forty days to avenge my father's murder. It was unbearable. "I will fight them, Father. I will destroy them for what they have done."

"I know you will, but for now, your mama needs you to

be strong. Can you do that? God would want you to do that."

"I don't care what God wants."

"What about doing it for your mama? She needs you, and I need you to be strong."

"Yes. Papa told me to be brave like Laskarina Bouboulina, and I will be brave."

"That's my Zoe. There will be tough times ahead. Tough times, but we must hold on to hope and our faith, and we will fight them off."

"When?"

"I don't know, but God will show us the way, and we will follow."

"What if God doesn't show us the way?"

"He will. I have faith in Him, and He will guide us."

"I don't have faith. If I don't have faith in God, what happens?"

"Oh, my child, don't worry. I have more than enough faith for the both of us. Together we will overcome this."

"I hope you are right."

"I'm right. God will see us through this darkness."

I didn't believe God was going to answer our prayers. Father H did, but he was a priest, so that made sense to him. God had lied to me, and I would never trust him again. God lied about my brothers, and he lied about my father. I would avenge their deaths rather than wait for God to act. What was it that Father H used to say in Sunday school? God helps those who help themselves. Well, we would soon find out if that was right or it was another lie.

CHAPTER 11

OCTOBER 16, 1941

FARSALA

Happy Birthday to me! It was my thirteenth birthday, and I had set off in the early hours of the morning to collect wood so we wouldn't freeze. I had suggested to my mother that we take one of the doors down and break it up into firewood but she didn't think that was a great idea. It was a genius idea to me because it meant I wouldn't have to go out in the snow. Reluctantly, I set out and I took my crossbow with me in case I found a rabbit, but there were none to be found. I collected as much wood as I could carry in a large sack and trudged back home.

As soon as I started walking down the road leading to the farm, I saw them. There was a large group of them and some were milling outside the gate leading to our farm. Useless thugs. I passed them without a word. I wasn't surprised to see the soldiers stealing our property. One of them snatched my sack and laughed as he walked away. The only thing that stopped me from flinging the rock at him was the look my mother was giving me. She was standing near the doorway.

"Now is not the time to be rebellious."

I wanted to ignore her plea, but I obeyed. My mother looked so worn out. Although I wasn't near her bedroom, I knew she cried herself to sleep every night. I fell asleep and dreamt of how I was going to avenge my father's death and how to ease my mother's suffering. When I wasn't thinking of new ways to resist the invaders, I was trying to starve off the hunger pains. I never thought of food all the time before the war. Now I did.

My father had prepared for war. We all took food and other items into the fields and stored them in the underground cellars Papa had made long before the war with the Italians. He knew what was coming. He and my brothers had created underground cellars to house food and other supplies. His grandfather did the same thing before the liberation from the Turks. Papa always said that soldiers need to be prepared for battle even during peace. My father was a veteran of the Great War. He fought with the Allied forces at Skra in 1918 and knew all about how to prepare. We had managed to survive so far because of what he had done in the year before the war.

Unfortunately for us, the food we had stored was not enough. We had shared it with our neighbors, and now we had none left. Mama tried to grow onions, leeks, and other things in the garden hoping the Italians would not steal them. I went hunting, but it was getting harder each day to try and kill enough food for us to survive on. Hunger and death were all around me. You can't keep Greeks down because we rise and fight back, but not if we're dead.

The Italians laughed and I was brought back from my thoughts about food and murdering the invaders. They must have known how much I hated them because I didn't think I was hiding it very well. One of the soldiers kept looking at me. He had dark curly hair and blue eyes. He couldn't be that much older than Stavros. I wondered how long it would take me to take Papa's gun, which was hidden nearby, and shoot them. I didn't want to die on my birthday, so I kept that idea to myself.

I was appalled by their brazen theft. I shouldn't have been because they did it all the time, but the unfairness of it all made me angry. Didn't the Italians have food? The country was starving. Severe famine had gripped the nation, and these fools thought they should steal what was left?

As I watched the soldiers I didn't have to wonder how our men had managed to beat them in Albania. They were dumb brutes. We had some luck because the previous day we had emptied the cellar. Mama said it was to organize it better. That didn't make sense to me since I don't think cleaning was something we needed to do. The cellar was filled with old furniture and clothes. Some of the soldiers walked into the barn, and moments later they came out with some of Papa's tools. One of them, the young one, looked back at me and winked. I wished I could have wiped that smile off his ugly face.

Greeks had to rise up like they did in 1821. This couldn't continue. There were whispers around the village that brave men and women were joining the Resistance.

There was talk about the partisans going up in the mountains and forming Resistance groups, but it was all whispers. I was ready to join them but first I needed to find them.

I wondered if those rumors were lies that someone made up to keep our spirits alive. You can't kill off hope, can you? You can't be brave and do nothing to force the enemy out.

So much for all my talk about Laskarina and bravery. I was not living up to the promise I had made to my father. What was I doing? I was making empty, worthless threats against dumb Italians. Words are meaningless unless you do something about it. I had to find out how to join the Resistance. There was a problem with my plan; I didn't know how to reach them.

It was late at night, and I had been thinking of all the horrible things that had happened since the war had started. Despite the curfew, I was outside while Mama and my aunties were in the house. I couldn't stand to be inside.

Life can change in the blink of an eye. Ten months had passed since the earthquake struck and Yiayia Maria and Arty were killed. Nine months since my papa lost his life. How different our lives were now; the fight to survive was a daily struggle. The famine was widespread and getting worse by the day. There were so many deaths—men, women and children. No family remained unscathed. I didn't know how much more of this we could take.

Stavros had told me the British were blocking the ships with the food we desperately needed. How did Stavros know this? It didn't make sense that an ally would do this. What did it achieve and what did it matter to the Germans if the food didn't reach us? Didn't they realize we were starving? Didn't they know that the Germans and the

Italians were not affected? Idiots. Had everyone lost their minds?

I hated the British, who had now betrayed us. They came to our aid during the earthquake, but I suspect they did it for their own reasons and not to help us. Not only couldn't they stop the Germans from taking our country, but they were killing us by not allowing the food to get to us.

Who was worse? The Germans or the British? When my stomach rumbled and I went to bed hungry, I blamed both of them.

I was about to head back inside and go to bed when I saw someone coming down the road. The travelers were either foolish or didn't care about getting shot after the curfew. I looked around to see if there were any patrols in the area. Luckily for whoever was out there, they would live through their stupidity. I lingered near the doorway, trying to see where they were headed and, to my surprise, there were another two people with him. It was definitely a man. He was tall and broad-shouldered, and as I watched him, I realized that I knew that gait.

"Mama! Come out here!" I said without screaming it out.

"Zoe, get back inside, child. You're going to get shot."

"Oh, no, you want to see this."

I heard my mother's sigh, and moments later, she joined me. I pointed to the mysterious group approaching the farm. It didn't take her long to figure out who it was. She was out and running toward them seconds later.

"Well, so much for not alerting the patrols," I said to myself and then ran after her. I arrived just as my mother was engulfed by her brother, Ignatius. We hadn't seen

Uncle Ignatius for ten months, and we thought he had died when he went to fight the Germans with Uncle Petros.

I didn't know the woman and girl that accompanied him, and it wasn't a good idea to talk too much out in the open. We quickly ushered them inside the house and closed the door.

My mother and uncle started talking at the same time, and I thought they should just sit down. One of them would have to take a breath at some point. I glanced at the girl, who appeared to be my age. She was stick-thin and looked quite ill. She sat quietly on the sofa.

I sat down next to her, and she tensed up, which I found strange.

"Hello, my name is Zoe."

My new friend didn't say anything at first. She just stared at me with fearful brown eyes and kept playing with the gold cross around her neck. "It's all right; you're safe here. Do you want to come into my room?"

She didn't respond, but I took her hand and she let me lead her down into the cellar. She clutched my hand, and I felt it shake. I turned on the lantern and motioned for her to sit down on my bed while I sat down on the floor and crossed my legs.

"Is this where you sleep?"

My new friend had an accent. She wasn't Athenian because I knew what they sounded like. Maybe she was from the islands.

"Yes. There aren't any windows, so no one knows you are here. I don't know if it's day or night when I'm down here."

"Where's your papa?"

I took a deep breath. Usually, when I was asked about my father, I would well up and tears would roll down my cheeks, but I tried not to do that to the girl. I was sure it wouldn't be helpful if I started crying.

"My papa died fighting the Germans." There. I said it and didn't cry. It was the first time in ten months. "What's your name?"

"Esther."

"Where are you from, Esther?"

Esther cast a worried look towards the stairs leading up into the house. "It's all right; your mama is safe, and so are you."

"No one is safe."

"It's safer than walking on the road so late at night. You must have been in a hurry to risk being out during curfew."

For a moment, I thought she wouldn't respond, and then she said, "Thessaloniki."

That piqued my interest. "I have cousins and an aunt who are in Thessaloniki! My cousins are Jewish, just like you."

The fearful eyes returned, and I sensed she wanted to bolt up the stairs. It wasn't hard to guess with a name like Esther that she was Jewish. The gold cross that sat in the hollow of her neck didn't fool me.

"It's fine. I figured it out by your name."

"I'm not allowed to say my name to strangers. I'm supposed to say 'Maria.'"

I groaned loudly and fell over to try and make Esther smile. I glanced at her, and she was smiling. "I have so many cousins named 'Maria,' everyone will think you're another one of them." Esther giggled and, for the first time, seemed to relax a little. I mentally patted myself on the head.

"Uncle Ignatius said you were funny."

"Did he say I was 'funny in the head' or 'funny, ha, ha'?" I asked, making Esther chuckle.

"I don't have red hair, so it might be a problem to pass off as another one of your cousins."

"Nah, half of us have red hair, and the other half have brown or black." I wanted to know why she had changed her name. So far, I knew she was Jewish and from Thessaloniki. I risked it and asked. "Why did you change your name?"

I could feel her fear. "Because I'm Jewish. I'm not really from Thessaloniki. I was born in Hamburg."

Ah. The accent was German. Esther didn't look German; more Greek than anything else. I waited for her to continue. I think she was expecting me to say something, but for once, I chose to stay quiet.

"You don't hate me, do you?"

That wasn't a question I had anticipated. "Why would I hate you? We just met."

"The Germans killed your father."

Oh. "No. I don't hate all Germans."

"I'm half German. My mother is Greek," Esther quickly added.

"I only hate the soldiers. You're not a soldier in disguise, are you?" I teased, causing Esther to give me a toothy smile. "I didn't think so."

"The Nazis killed my papa as well."

It was said so softly that it took me by surprise, and my heart ached all over. "We have a lot in common."

"Was your papa Jewish as well?"

I laughed. It wasn't supposed to be funny, but the way she said it, hoping that we had more in common that being Greek or half Greek and the same age, made me laugh. "Sorry, that's not funny. No, my papa was a Christian."

"Oh. I'm sorry."

I heard the door to the cellar open, and Esther bolted from the bed and hid behind my makeshift wardrobe. My mother came down, holding another blanket in her arm. I indicated where Esther had gone, and my mother nodded sympathetically.

"Esther, darling." Esther looked around the wardrobe and offered a shy smile. "You and your mama are staying the night. I have some soup for you and also wanted to give you a blanket so you will be warm. It does get a little cold at night."

A little cold? Try freezing cold, but we didn't want to scare Esther.

"Thank you, Aunty," Esther quietly replied while I took the blanket and the bowl from my mother.

"I'll sleep on the rug, and Esther will have my bed."

You would think I had ended the war and won us a million drachmas by the way my mother was beaming at me. She kissed me tenderly before she said goodnight.

"Don't talk Esther's ear off; they've had a long journey."

"No, Mama."

Esther and I looked at each other and smiled as my mother went back upstairs. The look on Esther's face when she saw the food had mirrored mine earlier in the evening. It was a cloudy soup of rice and beans.

"Have you eaten? I don't want to take food out of your

mouth." Esther offered me the bowl and at that moment she endeared herself to me. It was a loving, unselfish gesture.

"I already ate. You should have been here earlier. I would have picked out the beans and kept them aside for you if we had known you were coming." I half-joked because I detested beans. Esther giggled. I looked away while she was eating and made a bed for myself using the flokati rug and the blanket. I wondered how long it had been since she had a meal. By the time I turned around, the bowl was empty.

"You obviously like beans," I said and chuckled. I took the bowl from Esther and laid it on the step.

"How did you lose your father?"

Oh, that question again. "My papa was taking Australian soldiers back to their comrades, and he got killed by the Germans. How did your papa die? Was it in Thessaloniki?"

"No." Esther held my pillow against her chest and wrapped her arms around it. I sat back and braced myself against the wardrobe and waited.

"Have you heard of Kristallnacht?"

"That's a German word, and I don't know what it means."

Esther sighed deeply. "The translation would be 'Crystal Night,' and it happened in 1938."

"That sounds beautiful."

I must have said something wrong because Esther's brown eyes closed and tears ran down her cheeks. There wasn't anything I could do about it and I wasn't sure why it was wrong. "I'm sorry. I thought the name sounded beautiful."

Esther wiped her eyes with the back of her sleeve and took a moment to compose herself. "You didn't hear about what they did to the Jews?"

I shook my head and didn't have the heart to tell her that I spent most of my time drawing, reading novels, or playing with my friends. I had been shielded from the talk of war by my parents.

"When that evil man came to power, Papa said that we needed to get away from Hamburg because it would be bad for us, but we couldn't leave because my grandmother was ill."

"I've heard Hitler is a madman, and so are his soldiers."

"You don't really know how evil they are, Zoe. Last November, I was going to school. When I approached our synagogue, there was this mob outside screaming and throwing rocks at the beautiful stained-glass windows."

"Were they drunk?"

"No, they were Nazis. My friends and I ran past them, and we safely got to school. We were terrified because they were like rabid dogs. The school told us that we weren't going to have classes and that our parents were going to come and collect us."

"That sounds awful. What happened?"

"My mother came and took us home."

"Did the police come and arrest those crazy people?"

"A Nazi in Paris had been shot by a French Jew, and they took out their 'grief' on us. The Nazis set fire to the synagogues and the police did nothing to stop them."

I sat there, dumbfounded by the revelation. "Did this only happen in Hamburg?"

"No, all over Germany."

"Nazis attacked your churches, and the police did nothing?"

"They attacked people who were Jewish, and they broke shop windows, our homes as well as our synagogues. The police and firemen did nothing to put out the fires or stop the beatings."

"That's why it's called 'Kristallnacht.'"

"It was a night of broken glass all over Hamburg and the rest of Germany."

"What happened to your papa?"

Esther closed her eyes. "Papa went to find our rabbi despite Mama begging him not to go out. He wanted to protect our rabbi because he was a frail old man. Papa and the rabbi were murdered by the mob."

I sat in stunned silence with tears running down my face even though I didn't know the people who had been killed. We were both crying. I got up and went to sit next to Esther on the bed. I put my arm around her and held her as she sobbed. I knew the Nazis were heartless bastards, but I didn't know about Kristallnacht.

"Did you leave Hamburg with your mama?"

Esther nodded. "Mama is from Thessaloniki, and my grandparents told her to come home. We didn't have a lot of time and thought we would be safe from the Nazis in Thessaloniki."

"You were not safe because of the Germans invading, right?"

"Yes, but we were fortunate. The local priest took us to another Greek home, and the family there hid us until we could move to another house. I didn't know how we were going to escape, but the Lord always finds a way to help His people."

I was going to tell Esther what I thought of God and his help, but there are things best left unsaid. "Is that how you met my uncle?"

"Yes. Uncle Ignatius came to the house with another woman…"

"Ah, that must have been my cousin Ellie! She has red hair and green eyes like me."

"No, that wasn't her. This woman had white hair and black eyes. She scared me because she talked fast and waved her hands in the air a lot. I thought she may be a little crazy."

I chuckled. "That's Aunty Stella, she's not crazy…I don't think she is. She's a doctor."

"The two of them arranged for some men to meet us, and they took us out of the city by car at night."

"Where are you going to go?"

"I don't know, but Uncle Ignatius said that someone will be coming for us tomorrow."

The door to the basement opened, and we looked up. "Girls, time to go to sleep," my mother's voice rang out before the door was shut again.

I went over to where I had left my crossbow. "I'll have my crossbow with me while I sleep, and if someone comes in, I'll be ready to shoot any intruder."

"What if it's your mother?"

"I'll know if it's Mama. She makes a lot of noise and always finds the steps that creak."

Esther giggled and wrapped herself up with the blanket. We looked at each other and smiled. "We have the Lord to thank for so many good people helping us. Thank you, Zoe."

"I didn't do anything other than listening. Go to sleep now. You have a long journey ahead of you tomorrow."

I turned off the lamp, plunging the cellar into darkness. Esther softly cried herself to sleep, and I stayed alert until my eyelids were heavy and I eventually drifted off.

CHAPTER 13

MARCH 15, 1942

I truly hated the winter months. It was even more difficult since the occupation. Rain and snow fell in abundance; if the rain was food, we would have died from gluttony. Spring held some hope—not by much, but it was better than winter. It was still cold and, rather than go down to the river, I was perched on a ledge high up in the barn. While it wasn't the warmest place, I didn't want to be in the cellar. As I often did since Esther and her mother left us, I wondered what had happened to her. I asked Mama and she said it was best not to ask questions. That, of course, didn't stop me from thinking about it.

Uncle Ignatius and Aunt Stella were in the Resistance. I was surprised about Ignatius because he was a quiet fellow, but, as my grandmother used to say, it's the quiet ones that are the most surprising. And she would know since Ignatius was her son. I wasn't surprised to learn Aunt Stella was involved. I'm glad someone in our family was part of the Resistance. If only I could find out how I could join in.

MARY D. BROOKS

I tried to get information, but all I got was meaningless babble. I badgered Stavros for information, and he told me I was too young and I should shut up about it before I got myself killed. Was Stavros a coward? I never thought I would be saying that about him, but everything pointed to the fact he was not interested in the Resistance.

One night I couldn't sleep and decided to sneak out despite the curfew and my mother's orders. There was a full moon, and it cast a bright light across the valley. It was so beautiful that I wanted to sketch it but then decided that I would just enjoy the peace. The farmhouse cast long shadows and I hid behind the porch siding in case there were any patrols along the road.

I heard the front door quietly open, and a figure clad in black came out. It was Stavros. I watched him through the slits in the siding as he disappeared into the night.

Where was he going? Did we have another collaborator in the family? That couldn't be; Stavros wasn't like that, but then the war had revealed people to be not who I thought they were. Little did I know that I'd find out just days later what he was doing that night.

From my perch on a ledge in the barn, I saw one of our neighbors arrive and enter the house. Another ten minutes went past, and I saw yet another neighbor come by. It was like a dance, but I couldn't hear the music.

I counted ten that hadn't left and wondered what was going on. My curiosity got the better of me and I got down from my ledge and approached the kitchen door, but it was closed. My mother usually left it open, even in winter, so I thought she had probably gone out. Was I having a dream about the neighbors coming to the house?

I was about to turn away when I heard hushed voices coming from the kitchen. I leaned into the door and put my ear to it. It wasn't my imagination, after all. There were people in the kitchen. They were talking about someone who was in the mountains. It confused me as to why it was so secret, since we knew a lot of people had gone into the hills, but then the talk turned to the Jews. I had stumbled onto a Resistance meeting right under my nose! All this time I had been wondering how I was going to get myself involved and didn't know it was in front of me.

I stepped back in amazement. The voices belonged to my mother and Stavros! How didn't I know that my mama was involved? There was only one way to find out. I stormed into the kitchen and everyone reacted as if I had set off a bomb.

"Is everything all right, Zoe?"

Catching my mother, my aunts (the same ones who were supposed to be in the mountains), a few of my neighbors, and Stavros in a clandestine Resistance meeting was not going to make me feel 'all right.' I was extremely annoyed that I had not been invited to join.

"Why wasn't I included in this Resistance meeting?"

"Who said it was a Resistance meeting?" Stavros must have thought I was brainless.

I glared at him, and he had the good grace to look embarrassed. I was young, but I wasn't stupid. My mama was smiling at me. She was either proud of me for figuring it out or trying to come up with a way to calm my anger.

"Close the door, Zoe."

I glanced at my mother and did as instructed. When I returned to the group, the maps came out.

"What are you doing?"

"We are hiding Jews in the cellar in the northern fields." Mama didn't try to lie to me. What was the point? I already knew it was a Resistance meeting.

Stavros explained, "We have a family of five that has escaped from Thessaloniki living in the cellar."

It wasn't such a complicated problem that it required so many people. We could go over there and bring them out. I looked at the dozen pair of eyes staring back at me in puzzlement.

"Our northern fields?"

My mother nodded.

"Ah, so that's where you were going that night!" I turned to Stavros and pointed my finger at him. I turned to Mama, who was giving me one of her disapproving looks. "I couldn't sleep. I couldn't help it if I saw Stavros on his midnight run."

Stavros shook his head. "I told you that Zoe had seen me."

"You didn't see me!" I said incredulously.

"You forgot that if you can see through the slits, others can see you back."

"I thought you were a collaborator!"

"You did what?" Stavros' voice almost screeched. "Did you tell anyone else what you thought?"

"No! I wasn't certain!"

"Good, because I would be dead if you had!"

"You sound like a hysterical old woman! Calm down. I'm not the one keeping secrets!"

"The both of you, hush!" Mama raised her voice and

that ended our mini-battle. We glared at each other instead. "Zoe..."

I was very familiar with my mother's tone, so I turned away from Stavros. "That's why E..." I stopped talking when my mother's eyebrows shot up in a non-too subtle warning.

"Zoe, let's go inside your room to talk."

That was never a good sign. I followed Mama down to the cellar and she closed the door. We sat down on the bed, and Mama looked at me for a moment. "I want you to do something for me..."

"I want to be in the Resistance."

"Zoe..."

"I'm old enough. I'm only three years younger than Stavros, and he's at the table. Why can't I be?"

"You are already in the Resistance, my little one."

"No." I shook my head. "I don't mean trying to evade the Italians or throwing rocks at them. I want to be *in* the Resistance, just like Laskarina was. I want to fight."

"Zoe..."

"I'm a good shot. Papa taught me, and you know how good I am with my crossbow."

"This is different."

"Father H says that we must fight, and it's an eye for an eye..."

"That's not what Father Haralambos means about that scripture."

"Does it matter what he means? Papa told me to be like Laskarina, and that's what I want to do! The brave fight but cowards run. Isn't that right?" In my excitement, my voice may have risen a bit too much.

My mother didn't appear to be surprised or upset by what I was saying.

"Your papa and I knew this day would come. I know you can hunt and shoot', but what is out there is something eviler than you realize."

"I know it's evil. Esther told me about Kristallnacht. Do you know what that means? It's—"

"The Night of Broken Glass. Yes, I know what it was."

"You've been in the Resistance all this time and you didn't say anything! Even when I was begging you to find out how we could join."

I had a long-suffering and patient mother. She sat there and listened to me without interrupting. Once I stopped talking, she took my hand and held it.

"You have never seen what evil men can do. Kristallnacht is not the worst they have done or will do, and I pray to God every day that you may never know the truth."

"Is that why you cry every night?"

"I miss your papa and my boys every night, and I know you miss them as well."

"Isn't that even more reason for me to fight? Isn't that why you told me about the Spartan children and why we make promises and must keep them? Aren't we in a fight for our lives?"

"Yes, my darling, I did but–"

"Let me fulfill Papa's wishes. He said I needed to be brave and fight."

"That's not what he meant."

"He told me to be brave, just like Laskarina, and she was fighting for liberation. How am I going to be like her if

I don't fight? If I'm not in the Resistance, how do I do that?"

"I don't want you in the Resistance."

"Why, Mama? Am I not brave enough? What do I have to do to prove it to you?" I was quickly losing control of my temper, and I had become more determined than ever that I was going to convince my mother that I was ready.

My mother sighed deeply and took me in her arms. When I looked up, tears ran down her cheeks. I had made her cry, but this was more important.

"Zoe, if I lose you..."

"You're in the Resistance. What if I lose *you*? Did you think of that when you joined?"

Silence. My mother didn't say a word, and the longer the silence went, the less confident I felt that she was going to give in to my demand to join the Resistance.

"Please, say something."

"If I forbid you to join, you will do so regardless of what I say."

"That's not true. I will keep asking until you relent."

"You will never stop asking, will you?"

"No," I replied honestly. "I don't want to disobey you, but you taught me to be honest and I won't lie to you. I will never stop asking."

"You have left me no choice, Zoe. I don't want you to—"

"But—" My mother placed her finger over my lips to silence my interruption.

"Let me finish before you get upset by what you think I'm going to say. I don't want you involved, but I can't stop you. Papa and I taught you and your brothers to stand up for what is right."

I stayed silent as my mother's words sank in. It was true; my parents taught us to get involved if we saw injustice and help those who were in need. I doubt either of them thought that war would invade our home and bring us to where we were.

"I will refuse to die, Mama."

My mother smiled through her tears. "I doubt Hades will want to mess with you, little one."

"I promise you that I will do whatever I can to stay alive."

"Darling, don't make that promise. You won't be able to keep it. All I ask is that you are careful, run when you have to, and remember to pray to God for help."

Should I have told Mama that I no longer prayed to God for deliverance? I didn't think she needed to hear that right then. I nodded before being engulfed in her arms. She kissed the top of my head and wiped her eyes with the back of her hand.

"Can I go with Stavros to the northern field?"

"Not tonight. We need food to feed them and we don't have a lot. You and Stavros can hunt for our food. Do you want to do that?"

I was about to protest that I was now in the Resistance when I looked into my mother's face, which radiated love towards me. I smiled instead of complaining because she knew what I was going to ask.

"We are moving the Jews from the northern field and will eventually escort them into the mountains."

"Is that where Esther and her mother went?"

"Yes, they went into the mountains and from there I don't know."

"How will those in the fields...oh..." It dawned on me why my mother was involved in this. No one was going to carry maps in case they got caught. They had my mother for that!

She didn't need a physical map because she could remember whatever she saw and read. Mama was also an artist and could draw them the plan if they needed it. That was why she was a valuable member of the Resistance.

"We need to give the Jews food before we escort them into the mountains or they will starve."

"Well, we can't save them and then have them die on us."

My mother laughed, and this time I smiled because that *was* a joke, although it wasn't far from the truth.

"Has Uncle Ignatius gone back to Thessaloniki? What about Ellie and Angelos? We haven't heard from them. Are they being hunted as well?"

"I don't know where Ignatius has gone, and I haven't heard from Ellie or Angel."

My mother was not lying to me, but Papa always told me to listen when people speak because it's not what they say but what they don't say that matters. I gazed at my mother for a long moment.

"They're not safe, are they?"

"None of us is safe, Zoe. Now, I want you to go with Stavros. Promise me you will behave?"

"I promise to behave."

"A promise is a promise?"

"Well, if someone misbehaves and I have to break that promise, does that count?"

"You will do what you have to do, but be careful."

Well, I wasn't expecting that! I smiled at my smart mother and hugged her. "I promise to behave unless something happens. Can I take Papa's gun?"

"No. You can't fire a gun, or you will attract the attention of the soldiers. That gun belongs to your father and I want to bury it with him. It saved his life in the Great War."

"What use is a gun if it's buried in a grave? Papa doesn't need it. He's in heaven."

I saw Mama's eyes glisten, and I regretted saying anything. She took some time to compose herself before she looked at me. "You can't take the gun. If the Italians search you and find it, they will shoot you."

"If the Italians find us, they will shoot us anyway..." There are times when I wish I could punch myself in the mouth. That was one of those times. My stupid comment made my mother's tears roll down her cheek. "Don't cry..."

"Please, be safe. I can't lose you as well."

"I promise I won't die."

We both knew it was a promise I might not be able to keep, but I was determined to stay alive.

CHAPTER 14

MARCH 16, 1942

FARSALA

I was going on my first Resistance mission. That night, I was going to become a real partisan, and it filled me with trepidation, nervous energy, and, oddly enough, joy because I was finally doing something other than watching people die.

Our goal was to stay out of sight and not get shot. Getting shot was not high on the list of things I wanted to achieve now that I had infiltrated the Resistance. It was midnight when we set out to evade patrols. Stavros and I dressed in black; I wore my mother's black leather jacket and pants with a hat and boots. The coat was too big for me, but I made it snug by wearing a woolen sweater. It made me look twice my size. I was quite sure it looked quite comical; my mother tried not to laugh, but we both dissolved into loud laughter when I mimicked one of my aunties, who was a big woman and wobbled around. It wasn't respectful of my aunt, but making my mother laugh was my goal and it took my mind off my impending foray into the night.

The jacket was made of soft leather and, while I needed to grow into it, I hoped Mama would allow me to wear it more often. Papa had given her that jacket when he traveled to Turkey, and it was something she treasured. Especially now that Papa was gone.

Mama had applied grease to my face. I wasn't sure how that was going to keep me hidden, but she knew better than I did. Strapped to my back were my crossbow and a quiver of arrows. I was ready for the hunt.

Mama pulled me to her and put her arms around me. She held me, and I wondered if her heart was beating as fast as mine was. She pulled away and kept me at arm's length for a long moment. "You are going into battle for the first time."

"I'm going hunting, not to fight the Italians."

I'm not sure who I was trying to fool. Myself or my mother? Either way, it wasn't going to work because I was scared. I wished I still believed in God because I had the urge to cross myself and call on him to protect me. You can't call on someone you don't trust. Right?

Mama reached into her skirt pocket and brought out a wrapped object. Even before she unwrapped it, I knew that she was giving me my father's gun. She held it for a moment before she put it into my hands.

"Only use this if it becomes necessary to save yourself or Stavros. Don't use it for hunting."

"I won't. I will take it because this way Papa will be with me."

I couldn't see my mother all that well in the dark, but I heard her sniffing back tears. With a final kiss, she went back to the farm. I watched her walk away and wondered, for the briefest of moments, if I was ready for this. I felt unsettled but shoved my uncertainty down a pit and there it would stay.

Stavros came up to me and put his arm around my shoulders. "If we are careful, we will achieve our mission. Now, are you ready?"

I nodded and didn't want to admit I was feeling sick and wanted to throw up. I muttered to myself that warriors were never scared, and they didn't throw up. I wondered how we were going to get the rabbits back with us since we were walking to the fields. Were we going to drape the rabbits over our shoulders?

"Shouldn't we get a wagon?"

"No."

"How—"

"Shh. It's best not to ask too many questions."

As I followed Stavros, I wanted to use my crossbow to hit him over the head. I resisted the urge to do that. We kept walking and came to a clearing. On the opposite end was a soldier sitting at the base of a tree. He appeared to be asleep, his gun laid across his lap. I knew that face. He was the one that raided our supplies and winked at me.

I quietly withdrew the dagger that I had in my boot. It would be so easy to slit his throat. I took a few steps before I felt my hair yanked. I twisted around and slashed at Stavros, who sidestepped me effortlessly. I didn't intend to hurt him; I was just angry and let my anger get the better of me. Stavros dragged me by the arm into the brushes and slammed me against a tree.

"Have you lost your mind?" He said through clenched teeth. He didn't raise his voice above a whisper, but his face contorted with rage. "What use is killing that pig when we are on a mission?" Stavros was inches from my face, and he whisper-screamed his outrage.

I leaned in and whispered right back. "Killing Italians is also our mission."

"That's not *your* mission tonight, Zoe. You need to focus or I'm sending you home. Do you understand what I'm saying?" He spat out the words in my face.

"I wanted—"

"No, I don't care what you want. You are in the Resistance. It's war. You don't get to decide on what's next."

"I know it's war, but—"

"I said NO! It's not a game. When you take out a weapon, be prepared to use it. What were you thinking?"

"I was thinking I was going to get rid of an Italian."

"Are you *that* stupid? How close are we to the farm? Do you know who would die because YOU want to kill an Italian? Our family, Zoe. Your mother, our aunties. Is one miserable soldier's life worth the life of your mother?"

"You don't know that." That was a lie. Everyone knew that if you killed any soldiers, reprisals were swift and brutal.

Stavros let out an explosive breath and slid down the base of the tree. He ran his hand through his curly dark hair and sighed. "I told them you were not ready for this. I was right. You're impulsive and you have no idea what you're doing. You're young..."

"You're sixteen."

"I'm a man."

"You're a boy," I retorted and put my hand on his bicep. "I may not know what I'm doing, but I'm going to improve."

"You are incapable of following orders."

"You think I can't be a soldier, but I know I can. I promise to obey your orders."

I couldn't see Stavros's eyes, but I assumed he was glaring at me. Without a word, he got up and put his arm around my shoulders. "I don't want to go home and tell your mother I didn't protect you."

"Well, that wouldn't be good."

Stavros shook his head and pointed towards the pass. He followed after me once I passed him. We didn't say much to each other until we arrived at a clearing. Just as well, because I was angry with myself for being so stupid and not thinking about the consequences. Stavros was right. I was not ready.

I was tired and hungry by now, which didn't help my mood. I saw movement ahead and noticed Stavros had missed it because he was still walking ahead of me. I stopped and brought my crossbow forward. I positioned it on the ground and placed my foot in the stirrup while keeping an eye on the brushes. I squatted down and loaded the crossbow before I brought it back up and went down on one knee to steady myself before I fired.

"Stavros!" I yelled out, causing him to stop. He turned just as I was about to shoot into the brushes.

"Stop!" Stavros yelled and came running back. "Don't shoot!"

To my surprise, a figure materialized out of the scrub and guided a horse and cart out in the clearing. The man came forward and handed the reins to Stavros.

I didn't hear what they were talking about, but I felt foolish for having almost shot one of our compatriots. They glanced back at me for a moment before the farmer patted Stavros on the shoulder and left. That answered the question of how we would get the food back to the farm. I wanted the earth to open and swallow me whole. It was the second time that night I had almost made a grave mistake.

Stavros patted the horse before he slowly made his way back to me. He looked down at the crossbow and smiled. I wasn't expecting that reaction.

"You saw the movement before I did."

"I didn't think you saw it, and I wanted..."

"I know." Stavros put his arm around me. "That's why you are a huntress. You know what to look for."

"Why didn't you tell me that we were meeting a farmer?"

"I thought you knew, and that was why you didn't ask how we were getting the food back with us. You need to ask questions if something doesn't make sense to you."

"I did ask you and you told me to be quiet."

"I'm sorry; I should have stopped and listened to what you were asking."

"Shouldn't you have checked to see if I did know?" I shrugged but didn't expect Stavros to agree.

"We don't have time to talk about this now." Stavros went back to the horse and took the reins. We slowly made our way towards our northern fields at a faster rate now that we had a horse and cart. This field used to belong to my brother Michael. All the boys owned land because Papa wanted us to cultivate our land to appreciate what we had.

My thoughts of my brothers abruptly ended when Stavros hauled me off the wagon like a sack of potatoes and I fell to the ground. "Hey! Wh—"

Stavros put his hand over my mouth. "Shhh. Don't say a word."

I stayed mute, and Stavros must have wondered if that's all he had to do to shut me up. I occasionally followed orders. I also wasn't going to argue with him again because I suspected another hair yank was coming my way. Stavros maneuvered the horse and cart into the trees, and I followed him.

"Why are we stopping?"

"Didn't I say to be quiet?"

"You said I should ask questions."

Stavros sighed. "Not now, Zoe. We're here. Now is not the time to question me. It's time to focus on the mission. There's a group of soldiers ahead. They haven't seen us yet, or we would've had them come over. If we go straight into the fields, we will go right into an Italian camp. There's a group of maybe twenty soldiers at the edge of the field."

"Well, no, that's not a good idea."

"I thought you wouldn't like it. Do we have to go down the middle of the field to get to the forest?"

"Can I look?"

I moved to look around a tree, and Stavros pulled me back hard. I was about to swear when he put his hand over my mouth again.

"I told you to stick your hair under a woolen hat. Why didn't you listen to me?"

"I've been wearing this since I left the house, and now you see it? You're going blind!" I hissed back and pointed to the hat on my head.

Stavros cursed under his breath in Turkish, but I knew what he was saying because my brothers would do the same thing. He grabbed his black hat and pulled off the cap I was wearing. It appeared that a dark red cap was not the best thing I could have stuck on my head. Stavros tried to hide my curly hair under the woolen hat. I should have warned him that my hair tends to stick up no matter what I do to it. His curses made me rethink the plan of telling him anything.

"Next time we go out, you are going to paint that hair of yours black, do you understand me?"

"Well..."

"I mean it. You can be seen from Athens with that red hair." He grabbed a handful of my hair and tugged, which angered me. "Now, be careful. Tell me if we need to go through the field or if we can go around it."

I didn't say a word, because what could I say other than I was going to take my knife and stab his foot if he pulled my hair again? I was still angry when I yanked my arm away from him and approached the end of the clearing. Stavros was right— there were about twenty soldiers at the edge of the field.

"Zoe, what are we going to do? If we don't get our work done tonight, the Resistance won't be doing their job either. Now, what do we do?"

"We can't go down the center of the field because they

will see us. There isn't enough protection for us. We must go around the field to get to the trees and brush. That's where we can hunt without the Italians finding us."

"We may run into more patrols."

"Or we can go through the caves to the other side. It will take a longer."

Stavros brought me in and kissed me on the cheek. "The caves, of course! Now that is a great idea."

I was surprised when he lifted me off the ground and carried me like a bag of wheat over his shoulder. I was about to complain when I put my hand over my mouth. I heard Stavros' chuckle in the darkness.

CHAPTER 15

It did take longer than what we had initially planned, but it was the safest route. It didn't help that Stavros was leading the horse as if he was trying not to kill any ants. It was two in the morning and so eerily quiet. A gentle breeze rustled the leaves on the ground as we slowly made our way. We didn't speak when we entered the cave and quickly made our way through it before we exited to where we needed to be.

We arrived on the outskirts of the forest and led the horse and the cart through the brush. I remember Michael had a small barn to keep farm tools and other equipment. It was near the edge of the fields but out of the line of sight of where the soldiers had assembled. We made our way towards the barn.

Stavros guided the horse into a small clearing beside the barn. I jumped down from the cart. I could hear Stavros swearing under his breath that I should have waited. We didn't have a lot of time to hunt. Dawn would soon be upon us, and the patrols would start in earnest.

Stavros came up behind me and gently tugged my shirt for me to stop. He indicated his crossbow and then pointed to the barn. I didn't expect we would find anyone in there, but then we were in a war. We approached the barn, but we shouldn't have been worried. It was missing a door, and no one was inside.

Stavros tapped on his watch. "We can't hunt together. We need to split up." He put his crossbow at his feet and turned to me. I was taken by surprise when he cupped my face in his big hands. "Listen to me. Give me the gun your Mama gave you."

"No. I want to keep it with me."

"Give it to me; that's an order, Zoe."

Reluctantly, I took out the gun from my bag and gave it to him. "Go and hunt. Don't yell in triumph when you kill an animal..." Stavros pinched my lips shut before I had a chance to say anything. "I know how you are. You think it's a great victory, but you will alert the soldiers."

I sighed and nodded. I was too tired to argue with him. He let go of my lips just in time. I was going to bite him if he continued to hold them.

"All right, you go left, I go right."

I nodded. I felt a heavy weight settle on me as I made my way through the brush. Hunting was what I did with my brothers and father. They were always beside me teaching me the correct way to hunt for food. They taught me how to end an animal's life without causing it to suffer. Now I was on my own. I crouched down behind some thick brush and waited. I didn't pray for God to help me, but I prayed for my father to look out for me. I had more faith in my father than God. My stomach growled, but there was nothing I could do about it. Then I spotted it.

A fat rabbit. How in the world did the rabbit become so plump unless...oh, that was just wonderful...I was about to shoot a pregnant rabbit. Life was just unfair, Mrs. Rabbit. I raised my crossbow and waited until the rabbit was in position. I was ready to fire when I heard gunshots ring out, and the rabbit scampered away.

Goddammit. Stavros had told me not to shoot, and then he went and fired his gun. I should have stabbed his foot with my knife. I was getting up to confront him when I heard someone running and coming towards me.

I briefly caught sight of the woman before she slammed me and sent us both to the ground. She lay on top of me, and I looked up to find her brown eyes staring back at me.

"You have to protect me!"

I was on my back. How did she think I could protect her? I was going to try, but I couldn't do anything while I was lying on the ground. I pushed her off and sat up to find her looking back down the track. I have an excellent memory for faces, and I didn't recall ever seeing her around Farsala.

"Who are you?"

"My name is Sterina."

"Where are you from?"

"I'm Greek! That's all you need to know," Sterina snapped back, which didn't endear her to me.

"Did you fire the gun? You're going to get the soldiers coming towards us."

"I was running *away* from the soldiers! If I had a gun, I

wouldn't be running; I would be killing them! Let's get out of here; they are coming!"

Whoever was coming was making a lot of noise. Just my luck that Sterina and her pursuers would interrupt my hunting. Now we had a more significant problem than breaking curfew.

I took hold of Sterina's hand and pulled her into the thick brush. I didn't know where Stavros had gone, but I sure hoped he hadn't stumbled into the soldiers. Just as we hid behind the bushes, I heard a dog's bark and knew he was only moments away from discovering our location.

Goddammit. The hunt wasn't supposed to be so complicated! I tried to keep calm, but I was getting desperate. I pushed Sterina further into the brush when I caught sight of the enormous Alsatian dog. I saw him before he saw me, but my exit route was blocked. I had only one chance to survive his attack, and that was to shoot him. I glanced up the tree and wondered how fast I could climb it, but that would mean leaving Sterina down below.

I tried to load the crossbow, but my hands were shaking and I couldn't draw the string into place. I remembered my father's warning of 'squat and don't bend' when loading the crossbow. I took an arrow, went down on one knee, and waited for the dog. My mother's voice echoed in my head. 'Run if you have to.' I had nowhere to run and this was the stand I was going to take. The dog doubled back and found us. My heart was beating fast and it matched the throbbing in my head. I had to kill the dog or he would tear us apart. The dog started running and I fired when he was near enough that I wouldn't miss. My arrow hit him square in the chest. My heart broke on seeing his beautiful eyes close and the pain I had caused. He dropped to the ground and whimpered.

I hated myself for shooting this beautiful beast.

I hated the Italians for making me do this.

I had killed animals before, but this was different. It wasn't a clean kill, and the dog was in pain. I couldn't leave him to suffer. I just couldn't.

"I'm sorry, puppy." I caressed his head as he lay dying. He tried to snarl, and the fight in him was still there. I liked that about him. I reluctantly ended his life and dragged his body onto the opposite side of where we were. He was a magnificent dog and didn't deserve what I had done to him. I wanted to bury him, but the soil was too hard, and I didn't have anything to break the ground. I covered him with leaves and left.

The dog's death weighed heavily on me, but something else was wrong. I expected the soldiers to follow the dog, but they never came. Where were they? While I was wondering where they had disappeared to, the reason for their absence made itself known. I sniffed the air, and the unmistakable smell of burning wood ignited a memory in me that terrified me. My father, brothers, and I were caught in a bushfire when I was twelve and the smell of the burning forest was etched in my mind. I was alone in the woods, I didn't know where Stavros was, and my rising panic was going to get me killed. The situation was spiraling out of control. Sterina was crying and I was at a loss of what to do.

I could make a run for it out in the fields, but the dogs would catch me, and that would mean certain death. I could climb the tree, but what good would that do? The Italians had eyes, and they could look up and quickly find me. Not to mention the fire that would consume everything in its path.

"What are we going to do?" Sterina yelled at me. I wasn't sure why she was screaming. The problem had been caused by her running around in a forest with guards after her.

"Stop yelling at me!" I yelled back at her, but she was already running away from me. It was not the way I had expected the night to go. Like an idiot, I followed her. Why was I running after the screaming woman?

We pushed through some thick brush and came to a clearing. Right in front of us was a German soldier with his back to us. Could my night get any worse? Sterina gasped, causing the soldier to turn around. He was just a boy, not much older than me, and he looked terrified and promptly dropped his rifle. That made us three terrified teenagers in a burning forest.

Once the soldier got over his shock, he scrambled to pick up his gun. I fumbled for my crossbow only to remember that I hadn't loaded it. By the time I was losing control, the soldier had regained his and was coming after us.

"Halt! Halt!"

I didn't know what he was saying, but it sure wasn't friendly, judging by the sound of his voice. We tried to outrun him. Sterina screamed and shots rang out in quick succession. A bullet missed me and hit the tree in front causing the bark to splinter and hit me in the face. Sterina, on the other hand, was not so fortunate. She was shot in the head and lay dead on the forest floor.

My anger replaced my fear, and I ran behind a tree and removed the knife out of my boot. If the soldier wanted to kill me, then he would have to work hard to do it because I wasn't going to give up. The idiot was shooting indiscriminately and one of those shots was going to hit me sooner or later unless I killed him first.

I saw my opportunity when he came into view. I drew back my hand and threw the knife. It didn't go where I had planned, but it lodged in the man's thigh. The blood was gushing and he was howling in pain. I stood there like a statue watching the soldier trying to get his rifle and stop the blood at the same time.

I was confident he couldn't do both, so I loaded my crossbow. I saw the fear in his eyes. My heart was beating fast, and my hands trembled when I aimed my crossbow. He tried to reach into his blood-soaked boot and that's when I fired, but the arrow flew over his head and hit a tree. He was still trying to get his gun and I was trying to reload my crossbow. I managed to drop my arrows and they scattered.

I tried to calm myself, but it wasn't working. I heard my father's voice, 'Be brave just like Laskarina, little one.' I desperately loaded the arrow that was within reach and fired. To my horror, the bolt struck the soldier's rifle instead of killing him. He was so surprised he dropped the gun, which fired, and the bullet hit the ground in front of me.

I *was* going to die and soon if this farce continued. We were both inept. It was just a matter of who was going to kill the other.

The soldier screamed in defiance as he pulled out my knife from his thigh. He threw it behind him and got his gun off the ground, and I had nowhere to run to because he was blocking the way. My back was against a massive tree trunk, and I had lost all my arrows and my knife.

The soldier raised his rifle to fire, and I was determined not to die a coward. If he was going to kill me, he was going to see me looking at him. He pulled the trigger.

Click.

There *was* a God who looked after the stupid and even those who didn't believe in him.

Oh, dear God, I thought my heart had stopped. Moments later, the soldier looked dazed, and then he fell forward, dead. A bullet had struck the back of his head.

I stumbled back and leaned against the tree. I tried to get air into my lungs and felt the bile burn my throat before I threw up. I took several large gasps of air as the acrid smoke burned my eyes.

"Zoe!"

I turned around to find Stavros coming towards me. "Zoe! I told you..." He stopped when he passed the dead soldier. "Oh, sweet Jesus, I saw him coming after you and I had to fire, hoping I wasn't going to hit you. I thought for sure I had lost you." Stavros took me into his arms and held me. He kissed me on the cheek before he let go of me. I watched him drag the dead soldier into the thick brush.

"What are we going to do?" I asked. My voice sounded strange and it trembled a little.

"Strip him off his uniform, steal his boots, and get his gun; they are of no use to him now," Stavros replied as he started to strip off the man's uniform. He gave the soldier's boots and gun to me. "I told you to be quiet."

"It's not my fault! A woman came running at me."

"She was an escaped Jew."

"How do you know that?"

"How I know is not important right now. I'm not going to wait for the soldiers, Zoe. Come along." Stavros pulled me by my shirt, and I almost fell over my own feet while running after him. We managed to get to the cart and the horse before we heard more gunshots.

"The Italians are insane. They are burning the forest!"

"That was a German soldier that nearly killed you. There must be more Jews in the forest, and they want to burn them." Stavros hauled me onto the cart, and he led the horse out of the forest and away from the oncoming inferno.

Stavros reached into his boot and retrieved my knife. He handed it to me. "It landed a few meters from me."

The air was becoming difficult to breathe. Flying embers landed on the cart, and I stomped them out with my foot. I looked back into the forest where the trees exploded and thought of the Jews trapped in there. I could hear their screams now, and gunshots too. Maybe they would be saved from being burned alive by getting shot. I know what fate I would prefer. The Italians and Germans were vicious people and I would never forget their insane lust for blood.

I turned away from the carnage. We made good time getting away from the area. As Stavros led the horse around a corner, we looked back to find the forest wholly engulfed in flames. Luckily, the path leading to the forest was a dirt road, and it was open fields with no crops. There was no chance of the forest fire spreading because it would hit a natural barrier.

I looked down at my clothes, covered in blood from the

dog and the soldier. I wiped my hands on my shirt, but the blood couldn't be wiped off.

"Stav, I killed a dog and buried him under the brushes..." I found myself unable to finish my sentence. I welled up, and tears streamed down my face for a dog I didn't know. His life was worth more than the miserable son of a bitch who had tried to kill me. It was worth much more.

Stavros slowed down the horse as we neared the farm. He turned to me and put his arm around me. "There will be more of that before this nightmare ends."

I wiped my eyes with the back of my hand.

I'm in the Resistance, and I must be like Laskarina.

I must be brave. I must be like Laskarina.

I must be brave. I must be like Laskarina.

I must be brave.

I chanted under my breath. It became my war cry. I must be like Laskarina. I must be brave. My eyes welled up again on seeing my mother standing at the gate, but I willed myself not to cry.

CHAPTER 16

Do mothers have a mysterious way of knowing things? It seemed that way. I knew Stav hadn't told her what happened because he didn't have time to say anything to her before he brought the horse into the farm. Mama was waiting for us; she must have been awake this whole time, and when I looked back towards the forest, I could see the flames and smoke billowing up into the heavens. Mama didn't say a word; she just pulled me to her embrace and hugged me until I felt like she was trying to absorb me into her. After I reassured her multiple times that I was all right, she drew a bath for me. I stank of the smoke from the fires, and I couldn't get the clothes off me quick enough. I hated the smell which only accentuated my disgust. I was so tired that I almost fell asleep in the bathtub, but I forced myself out of the tub and went down to the cellar. I don't remember falling asleep. I woke up still smelling the smoke.

I heard my mother's voice. She was angry, and whoever she was directing her anger at was not talking, because all I could hear was her voice. I winced when I realized Mama was yelling at Stavros. It wasn't his fault that Sterina ran into me or that I found the soldier. Mama was blaming him for all of it, which was unfair. I needed to tell her the truth.

Silence descended in the house, and I heard the back door open and close. It sounded like Stavros had been banished from our home until Mama could control her temper.

When I finally got out of bed and walked into the kitchen, Mama was trying to make some food with the meager amount of ingredients that we had. She stopped what she was doing and wiped her hands on a hand towel. She put her arms around me and held me until I felt I couldn't breathe.

"I can't breathe."

She sighed and led me to the sofa. "I am so proud of you. Papa would have been so proud of you. You're our brave soldier."

"I didn't do anything. I let the poor woman die…"

"You didn't let her die. You tried to protect her."

"I was useless. I didn't know how to protect Sterina, and she died. Did Stavros tell you about the soldier? Was that why you were yelling at him?"

"Stavros' job was to protect you. His job was to hunt with you and not let you go off on your own."

"It was easier to hunt separately. The soldiers were at the edge of the field, and if we hunted together, we might have attracted more attention."

My mother sighed heavily. Her emerald-colored eyes were glistening when the light hit them. She appeared to take a moment to compose herself. "The last thing I wanted you to do was to engage the enemy. You are not ready to go up against trained soldiers."

"Sterina was my age. Was she too young as well?"

"No, that's not what—"

"Whenever I got scared, you told me about the Spartan children and how brave they were. I didn't need to be brave in peacetime, but I need to be brave now. I need to learn how to fight."

"No."

"I can't confront another soldier and not know what to do if I lose control of my weapons."

"The thought of you putting yourself in harm's way breaks my heart. We have lost your brothers and your papa...I can't lose you."

"You won't. I will learn how to fight, and I'll become better at—"

"At killing? No, Zoe. I don't want you to be a better killer."

"You are putting yourself in harm's way by being in the Resistance. Why can't I?"

"You're too young and I made a mistake."

"Remember when you told me the story of the French girl, Joan, who led an army? Remember that? You told me she was my age."

Mama was used to my stubbornness. I was determined to stand my ground because we were in a war for our survival. I was determined never to be in a position where I was helpless against a larger opponent again. I had been lucky the previous night, and I feared that I wouldn't be so fortunate if I found myself in those circumstances again.

"I thought I had lost you when I saw the fire." Mama

held up her hand to forestall my considerable objections. "If you want to learn how to fight, I will ask a woman I know to come and show you."

"What woman? Do I know her?"

"No, you don't. The woman is a local commander of the Resistance and has been helping our Allies and the Jews to escape."

"She's not doing a good job then. Sterina and many other Jews were murdered in the forest fire last night."

"The Jews escaped from a convoy that was ambushed by the Resistance."

That's why I hadn't recognized Sterina. She wasn't from Farsala. That brought up another question. "Where were they being sent?"

"Thessaloniki."

"That's why they ran into the forest." It all started to make sense. "When can you talk to this commander? I want to learn how to fight." I didn't think we had the luxury of time for me to get better at fighting with soldiers. I'd have to practice.

"I will contact her, but it's going to take some time."

I didn't have time, but there wasn't anything I could do about it. After Mama gave me a kiss and a hug, she gave me Papa's gun back.

"Stavros saved my life using Papa's gun."

"I know. Stavros told me what happened. Your papa protected you last night."

"I will keep his gun with me."

"No, you must bury it with him. Please, I don't want you to have it. It's old and far too heavy for you."

I didn't think it was heavy, and I didn't understand why

I needed to hide the weapon. Every firearm was useful, even if it was old, and I was going to bury one? Mama said that it was one of Papa's last requests—he wanted the gun that had saved his life buried with him. That gun had saved my life as well.

CHAPTER 17

LAMBROS GROVE

My goal that afternoon was to grant my father his wish. I hadn't slept much', but I was determined to get it done. As I walked along the dusty road leading to the cemetery, I spent some time thinking about the soldier who had died in front of me. I didn't feel anything other than joy that it wasn't me who ended up bleeding on the ground or being consumed by fire. Was that normal? Was I supposed to feel something for the invader, even if he was close to my age? I'm a hunter and I've killed before, but the death of the dog affected me more than the soldier's death.

Then there was the fire. I shuddered at the thought of flames eating away at my flesh. I shook my head to try to get the image of the fire that had almost caught us out of my mind. I remembered the soldier's blue eyes as they widened in surprise when he saw us. He was bigger and stronger than me, but he wasn't fast enough. Stav said that there would be more like him that I might have to fight and kill. We were in a war, and this was what Laskarina had faced. Being brave like Laskarina was hard, and I wondered how she had battled the Turks and come out on top. I had survived my first battle by sheer luck. I was fortunate even though I was unprepared, but that wouldn't happen the next time. I had to be ready, and I had to learn how to defend myself.

I was terrified that night, and still was long after the mission had ended. Not as scared as Sterina, but then I'm not a Jew running through a forest with the Italians after me. Why didn't the Jews take up arms and shoot the bastards? Why did they allow themselves to be herded into those camps? I wasn't sure why the Italians and the Germans hated the Jews so much. It didn't make a lot of sense to me.

I stopped walking. Uncle Yiannis's words about Ellie's faith came back to me. 'They are not like us. The Jews murdered our Lord, and Ellie has turned into the devil's child.' That's what he had said about my beloved cousin and her choice to marry a Jew. Were the Jews different from 'us'? Do you kill people just because they are different?

I didn't know a lot about Hitler, but what I did know is that he had declared war and invaded most of Europe. I wasn't entirely sure how the Greek Jews fit into this madness or why they were hunted like animals.

Before I arrived at the cemetery, I saw the undertaker and his cart far off into the distance. Father Haralambos was with him. It was easy to spot the priest because of his long flowing black robes. They were busy men those days.

Kirios Grigori and Father Haralambos took the bodies out to a field because the town cemetery had run out of space. There were so many dead. Whole families had perished and were in the same plot. Father H prayed for them, but I wasn't sure why—they were gone, and it was too late for them.

My papa was buried in the Lambros Grove, and that's where I was headed. Everyone knew where the Lambros Grove was. You could see it for miles because of the large gnarly trees just inside it. I'm not sure how old those trees were, but they stood like sentinels. I had spent quite some time sitting on one of the limbs of the tree I called Goliath. It was a pretty place for a cemetery.

Lambros Grove wasn't a real grove but more of a family burial ground. Papa had decided that we needed a family plot that wasn't going to be disturbed. It wasn't the way it was done—to bury the dead for longer than three years. Usually, the dead were unearthed, and their bones put in small boxes. I shuddered at the thought of someone putting my bones in a box.

My father chose that area because it was peaceful and overlooked the mountains. He must have hated the idea of small boxes as well. Kirios Grigori looked after it because Papa had been kind to him when his wife died, and he had never forgotten my father's kindness. That's what I loved about living in Farsala—people cared about one another. With the war raging all around us, it was essential to care about your compatriots, because if you didn't, what else was there? Betrayal is never the answer, and it would only lead to death.

I approached Papa's grave, and an overwhelming

sadness engulfed me when I knelt in front of it. My father had given his life to save others. At the funeral, Father H read from the Bible, where it says that no greater love has one man than to lay down his life for his friends. My papa was honorable and courageous. Father Haralambos' words were beautiful, but I would have preferred to have my father alive. It was getting late, and if I wanted to beat the curfew, I would have to get home soon. I dug into the ground and created a hole big enough to bury the gun. I covered it up and placed some dry leaves over it.

I stopped in front of my Yiayia Maria's grave and took out a drawing I had created for my grandparents. I dug into the topsoil and buried the artwork before I visited every gravesite but left Arty's grave last. I sat cross-legged next to her grave and looked at the tombstone of a girl who had been taken sixty years before her time.

"I went on my first mission with Stav. I wish you had been with me. Did you see I renamed my crossbow? Yes, yes, I know you want me to call it Little Bow, but that's not going to happen." I smiled and could almost hear Arty's laugh. "I renamed her 'Artemis' in your honor. The girl who never wanted to hunt has a crossbow named after her." I chuckled. "I will avenge your death as soon as I learn how to fight. Do they allow God-haters up there?" I held back the tears that threatened to fall and patted the soil.

Even though the sun was setting, I found myself unwilling to leave the cemetery and decided to climb one of the trees. I sat back against the trunk and wondered what I was going to do next. My thoughts turned back to why they had set fire to the forest. A few Jews escaping from where they had put them was not a reason to torch an entire forest.

I thought the Germans had taken control of Thessaloniki and up north, but they were down here now. Why? What did it mean that the German thugs were here? For the Jews, it meant death. What about the rest of us?

"Fermare! Fermare!"

I turned towards the sound to see an Italian soldier running through the field. I wasn't sure why he was yelling for someone to stop because I couldn't see anyone. He kept on shouting and ran towards the other side of the field. I had been trying to learn Italian since they arrived so I could understand what they were saying. He was too far away to see me, so I doubted he was yelling at me.

It was just another crazy Italian until I caught sight of someone just outside the grove. They were trying to hide behind some fallen logs.

"Come this way!" I cried out in Greek, hoping the soldier who had passed his quarry didn't hear me. The man looked up at me, and I kept on gesturing for him to cross into the grove. He looked scared and hesitated.

I urged him to come over, and he finally stood up. I didn't know what I was going to do now that he had trusted me, but we would go back to the farm and Mama would know what to do.

I was climbing down from the tree when I heard the gunshots. I jumped down onto the ground and leaned around the tree to find the Italian soldier had backtracked and shot the man. He lay there in the field with the soldier over him. He had been murdered only a few feet away from me.

I cursed myself for leaving my crossbow at home because I could have used it to kill the murderous thug. Yet another time when I acted before thinking—I picked up a rock and threw it at the soldier.

The rock hit him on the helmet and didn't do any damage, but he saw me and his face contorted in rage. Now I was in real trouble. I reached into my boot for my knife, and to my horror, I realized I had forgotten to bring the blade as well!

I was facing death again. The soldier fired at me, but he hit the tree instead. I could run out of the grove, but he would shoot me. I could run the other way out of the orchard, but there might be other soldiers nearby. I was running out of options because the soldier was heading my way. I could hear him swearing, and I made a run for it.

The Italian spotted me and fired again, and I was sure the bullet whizzed past my ear as I ran for my life. I managed to hide behind my grandfather's headstone, which was more prominent than the rest. I had no options left, and the light was fading. The only way I was going to survive this encounter was to run into the soldier and surprise him. I could hear him coming, and if I looked around the headstone, I would get a good idea of how far I needed to run to barrel into him.

I counted to three and peeked. The soldier was looking away from me. I bolted from behind the headstone at full pelt. I ran into the soldier but I just bounced off him. I wasn't a match for his bulky build.

He smiled down at me, and I was looking at the barrel of his rifle and the end of my life again. I had to stop trying to get myself killed. For a moment, he took his hand off the gun and waved at me. I wasn't going to die, dammit. I felt the gravel that lay just under my hands. I grabbed a handful and threw it with all the force I could muster into his face. I had enough time to stand up while the soldier was yelling, and I ran past him and out of the grove. The yelling and gunshots followed me, and I knew I had to run fast or I wouldn't be able to cheat death again.

I sure hoped he ran out of bullets because I was getting tired. We left the field, and I bolted for the nearest forest of trees. At least this way I could hide and try to get my breath back. I stopped because suddenly I couldn't hear the soldier. If I looked around the tree I was hiding behind, I might be spotted. I took the chance, and to my horror, the soldier was right there. He grabbed my hair and slammed me into the tree.

My god, that hurt! I hit that tree with such force that I felt it to the marrow of my bones. I was about to die, and my short-lived Resistance activities were going to go down as the worst in history. He threw me on the ground and pointed his gun at me.

I took a deep breath and waited for the end. There was a gunshot, and the soldier fell on top of me. I started screaming like a frightened little girl when I saw boots near my head. I was going to die.

CHAPTER 18

There are days when it's best to stay in bed with the covers over your head. I should have spent that whole year like that. My head was throbbing, and I was bleeding from where I had connected with the tree. I could taste blood in my mouth and spat at the dead soldier. One thing you should never do—spit on someone who is lying on top of you. Like spitting into the wind, spitting up is never a good idea.

I had another problem; his comrades had found us. I started to protest loudly and tried to hit out when someone with a firm grip took hold of me. I saw a flashlight and what seemed like a dress. I thought my header into the tree must have loosened something up there.

"Zoe, stand still and stop fighting!"

I knew that voice! The flashlight turned away, and she put it up on her chin and grinned.

"Ellie!" I almost cried from happiness. I have never

hugged someone so fiercely as I did then. My head hurt and my body ached, but my soul rejoiced on seeing my tall, beautiful cousin. Standing next to her was the manliest looking woman I had ever seen. She was wearing a black dress and thick black boots, but there was something wrong with her face. She had it covered, and I could barely discern her eyes.

Ellie turned me away from the woman and put her arm around me. "You're bleeding, but it doesn't look too bad. I'm sure the tree is suffering more."

"What are you doing here?"

"That's a question I can't answer right now. We need to get out of here and back to the farm before your mother's hair turns white."

"Did Mama send you to find me?"

"She did."

"I bet Laskarina's mother didn't send anyone to look for her." Ellie put her hand over my mouth and shut off the flashlight. We quickly made our way to the thick brush and hid. I could hear voices; again, German and Italian. They would surely find the dead soldier if they came any closer.

To my surprise, the strange woman took off her scarf, and my eyes widened. Either my head knock into the tree had been worse than I thought or that was a man in a woman's dress. I was going to whisper to Ellie, but she kept her hand over my mouth. I watched as the she-man took out his gun from under his skirt. It was one of the most inventive ways to carry a weapon that I had seen.

The voices were getting louder, and my heart was thundering in my ears. They were almost upon us when the she-man stood and took a few steps sideways from us. He didn't break cover. The gunshots sounded so loud that I was sure we were going to have more soldiers come running towards us. The enemy soldiers dropped dead only meters from my dead Italian.

Ellie and this man began talking, and I realized they were speaking English. Despite my fear, despite everything that had happened, my heart leaped for joy because I knew who that man was—he was an Australian soldier. I recognized his accent, and I wanted to hug him.

Ellie went down on her haunches and smiled. "That's Sergeant Barry."

"He makes an ugly woman," I blurted and hoped Barry didn't know Greek. His chuckle as he dragged the dead soldiers into the thick brush told me he did. The danger was over, and all I wanted to do was go home, pull the blanket over my head, and stay there.

Then I heard someone coming, and they were not making a lot of noise. There was a muffled sound, and I knew it wasn't an animal approaching us.

Ellie left my side and pulled out her gun. She joined Barry, and they were about to open fire when they spotted their comrades coming into the clearing. I almost passed out from holding my breath. I sat back on the ground and sucked in some air. My heart was still racing and my head throbbed.

Ellie came over to me and smiled. "You're having quite an adventure. We need to get you home."

"Why are you in Farsala? Why aren't you up in Thessaloniki? Where's Angelos?"

"It's not the right time to play catchup with the family. We must get out of here." Ellie pulled me to my feet, but I was so dizzy that I braced myself against a tree. Just as I was about to have another go at standing, I turned and threw up, right on top of the dead soldier. Then everything went dark.

CHAPTER 19

FARSALA / ATHENA'S BLUFF

I woke up feeling like someone was sitting on my head. I wished that was the case because then I could shove them off. I felt awful and I just wanted to stay in bed. I lay there wondering how I could be so inept and useless. It was a miracle I hadn't killed myself so far. I may never get another chance and the third time would be the last.

I could hear voices outside my room. One distinct voice stood out above all the others, and that voice belonged to my uncle Petros. My beloved uncle Petros! That's why Ellie and Angel were here. Uncle Ignatius was here as well! This was the best present anyone could give me. I could ask Ignatius about Esther and her mother and see if they had made it to safety.

I had missed Ellie so much... It was a sad day when she and her Angelos decided to move to Thessaloniki to be closer to his parents. The last time I had seen her, other than the previous night, was when she and Angelos visited us during Easter just before the war. They didn't celebrate Easter with us, but it was a family occasion, so they came down and ate some lamb with us. I wanted to ask Ellie if she had received my artwork. She was a pagan Jew. I didn't understand how that worked but I didn't care. All I cared about what that she was here and soon I would see Angelos.

Papa always said that it was my crazy aunty Stella's influence on Ellie that made her turn to the worship of a mythical goddess. I bit my tongue, of course, but isn't God a mythical God? That thought was best left in my head because I would be subjected to Mama's lecture about God and why it was necessary. The last thing I needed was a sermon about faith.

I got out of bed and expected to be dizzy, but surprisingly, the world did not spin. I quickly dressed and practically bounced into the living room.

Uncle Petros rose from his chair and approached me. He took one look at me and smiled. "My goodness, ZoZo, falling out of a tree is not good for you!" He just loved to tease me and called me a nickname that only the family used. I jumped into his arms. He smelled like my father, and I had the overwhelming urge to burst into tears, but I didn't. You can't hug someone and then cry—that would be rude. I suddenly realized that his greeting was a little odd. Did he say I had fallen out of a tree? I didn't drop out of a tree. I have never fallen out of any tree.

"I'm glad you are up because we were wondering if you

had turned into sleeping beauty!" Uncle Ignatius' booming laugh filled the room and he also hugged me.

"I didn't sleep that much!" I joked and wondered if that was true. Everyone seemed to think so, but then my brain could be playing tricks on me. "Have you heard how Esther and her mama are coping?"

Uncle Ignatius looked at me with a puzzled look on his face. "I don't know who you are talking about. Who is Esther? That knock on the head did a little bit of damage up there." He gently tapped me on the nose.

Huh? Either I was losing my mind or Ignatius had lost his. I glanced at my mother, who wasn't paying any attention to me but rather fussing over some cakes she had made. Deciding not to embarrass myself any further, I turned to Uncle Petros.

"If it wasn't for Ellie last night…"

"Ellie? Ellie isn't here, Zoe; she's in Thessaloniki with Angelos and Aunty Stella."

Huh? No, she wasn't. Had I dreamed of getting rescued by my cousin? Regardless of my mental state, I was determined to correct him on his assertion that Ellie was not in Farsala. "No, Uncle, Ellie saved me from an Italian soldier last night."

Petros smiled. "No, no, she is in Thessaloniki. You probably dreamed it all."

I was confused. Had I dreamed about Ellie and the soldier? Were Barry and the other Resistance members a dream? I couldn't have imagined the whole thing. Surely someone was lying because I was *not* losing my mind and I was NOT dreaming this strange conversation.

Mama came over from the kitchen. Her smile didn't

reach her eyes, and that worried me. Her eyes appeared bloodshot, and I wondered if I was the reason for that.

"Were you crying?"

"No, darling. Aunty Flosso had some onions..."

My mother was terrible at lying. Awful. I let it pass because she *had* been crying and I was the reason. Again. She put her arm around me and kissed me on the head.

"How's your head?"

"I think it's still there, but it looks like it's not working properly," I joked, knowing she must have been anxious. I expected her to join me in the joke, but she just smiled. Something was definitely wrong. Everyone else had gone back to talking amongst themselves and I leaned in to whisper to my mother. "Where is Ellie?"

"Ellie? Your cousin Ellie?"

My mother was the one who had sent Ellie to find me and she was now acting as if this was a figment of my imagination. Either I was still asleep, or someone had hit these people on the head making them forget Ellie and Esther.

"Um..."

"Didn't Uncle Petros say that Ellie is in Thessaloniki, darling? That knock to the head must have done some damage." Mama laughed but it wasn't a genuine laugh.

"Yeah, maybe I dreamed her." Not really, but what was I going to say when I knew Mama was lying to me? She never lied to me. Usually, she would tell me that she couldn't reveal the information to me. I'd be curious for a short while, but then I'd find something else to occupy my time until Mama was ready. Three things were sacred in my family (what was left of my family)—no lying, no secrets, your word is your bond. My parents instilled those three things into my brothers and me. Now Mama was lying. The world was indeed coming to an end.

"I'm glad you're up and are not running a fever anymore."

Fever? What fever? I didn't have a temperature. I got hit on the head by a tree. What was wrong with my mother and my uncles?

"I have some oil to send up to your Aunty Athanasia; let me get it for you."

What? Aunty Athanasia wasn't my real aunt, but a dear friend of Mama's who was like family to us. The problem was that Aunty Athanasia was dead. She had died a couple of weeks before, and now my mother wanted me to take her some oil? Why? I didn't think the dead needed light while they were in a grave or in heaven or wherever they go.

Everyone else continued to chat amongst each other and didn't pay attention to me while I was standing there thinking the world had gone even crazier than it was. Mama came back with a lamp.

"Let me walk you out." She put her arm around me and led me to the door. I was going to ask her if everything was alright, but I looked into her eyes and quickly shut my mouth. I knew that look.

We walked outside, and one of the old gossipy old women was hanging up some washing. It was a bright sunny day, which only made me wince. My mother stuck a hat on my head. It wasn't what I was expecting. Neither was the hug she gave me or what she whispered in my ear.

"How's your head?"

"Confused," I replied making my mother smile.

"Avoid the patrols on the way to Athena's Bluff and stay there until I send Stavros to come and get you."

That's all she said. I decided it was wise for me to obey and not ask any other questions. When Mama was ready to tell me, then she would tell me. I kissed her goodbye and set off down the road. I stopped and looked back—I had forgotten to get my crossbow. I was in two minds, whether I should go back or continue on my way. My problem was solved when Stavros came out holding my crossbow and my knife.

"Aunty Helena thought you might want to take these with you when you go hunting," he said a little louder than he should have. These people needed to get their stories straight. We used to joke about Athanasia's name that she was immortal. Maybe there was truth to that, and she wasn't dead. Either I was taking dead Aunty Athanasia some oil to Athena's Bluff, or I was going hunting. I couldn't do both.

Stavros gave me my weapons, but he didn't look me in the eye, which again was strange.

"I'll keep an eye out for Athanasia's ghost while I'm hunting," I muttered just loud enough for him to hear. He tried to stifle a laugh as he walked away.

I wasn't up to a long walk so soon after rampaging through the forest and kissing a tree with my head. I was not feeling well; the heat was getting to me, and the last thing I wanted to do was trudge up a mountain. Mama told me she wanted me to avoid the patrols, and the only way was to take a different, much longer route to Athena's Bluff. I was confident that the Italians wouldn't be bothered patrolling near the caves. The mountain surrounding

Farsala had an extensive cave system. By the time I reached the caves, I was ready to pass out. I hadn't taken any water with me, which was stupid. I knew there was a rock pool nearby, so I made an effort to find it. The Italians had a habit of poisoning the water supply. These people were evil, and when I finally worked out how to kill them without nearly killing myself, I was going to seek vengeance like they had never felt before.

If I drank from the pool I might end up dead from poison. If I didn't drink I might end up dead from thirst. I crossed myself and hoped that God did indeed protect the stupid. I swallowed and found myself still alive. That was the best news I had had in a long time.

I entered the caves, and it was dark until I used the lamp to light my way. Poor Athanasia would have to do with less light. I had been in the caves many times and I knew my way around. I turned towards the tunnel that led to the other side of the mountain. I started to sing to myself as I walked down the musty smelling cave. I stopped when I heard a scraping noise.

Someone was in the cave with me. I wasn't sure where the sound had come from. I closed my eyes and listened just as my father taught me when we were hunting. I could hear someone breathing. I put the lamp at my feet and brought the crossbow forward. Whoever was in the cave with me was going to die.

CHAPTER 20

My heart was beating so fast I was sure my quarry could hear it. I gripped my crossbow and prepared to fire. I stepped away from the oil lamp and headed into the darkened area of the cave. I should have waited for whoever was there to come to me just as my papa had taught me, but whoever it was in that cave was not armed—if they were, they would have taken a shot at me. I stopped when I saw the dark shape move and raised my crossbow.

I fired.

A child's high-pitched scream echoed in the cave, sending me to my knees in shock. I had killed a child! Damnation! I was going to hell. I was cursed. I sat on the ground, bowed my head and tried to calm my heart, which was about to gallop out of my chest and into the cave with the dead child.

"Don't shoot."

I looked up to find a dirty looking face looking at me. I was stunned and surprised to find that my aim was so bad, but I didn't care. I was just thankful that the child was still alive. The little girl was no more than five years old, but then with the famine ravaging the country, she could have been older than she looked because of how thin she was. We were all skinny except for the Italians and Germans.

"What are you doing here?"

"Mama told me to run."

"You ran into a scary cave?" I got up slowly because I didn't want to scare the child any more than I already had. "Where's Mama?"

"I don't know."

"What's your name?"

"Sarah Michalidis."

I didn't know any families called Michalidis. She wasn't from Farsala because I didn't recall seeing her. I beckoned her to come to me, and she was reluctant. I couldn't blame her since I had just shot an arrow at her.

She eyed me for a long time and then must have decided that I wasn't going to shoot again because she came into the light. I gasped when I saw her tiny body covered with scratches. She wasn't wearing shoes, and her feet were bruised and bleeding. I opened my arms, and she walked into my embrace. She weighed nothing as I picked her up.

I took her to the ledge and placed her on it while I removed my shoes. They were going to be too big for her, but at least she was going to have something to protect her feet. I had another pair of shoes at home.

"They're big." Sarah giggled when I put the shoes on her.

"You'll be able to show Mama, and you can flip-flop to her."

Instead of making the child laugh, I made her cry. What had I said that made her cry? "Big girls don't cry."

"I'm not a big girl."

"Where are you from?"

"Piraeus."

No. Surely that was wrong. How could Sarah be from Athens and be hiding in a cave in Larissa? That wasn't possible. I was about to question her again when I heard voices and someone approaching.

"Dear God, that is not the sound of a child's footsteps." I quickly picked up Sarah and hid her behind the boulder. "Shh," I said and got behind the rock myself. I was going to shoot whoever was coming, and I prayed that my aim was straight because it wasn't just my life at stake.

Just as the person was about to come around the corner, I stood up, took aim, and fired. To my utter disgust, the arrow hit the rock wall and bounced off. I screamed in frustration at being so inept.

"Dear God, Zoe, you're about to turn my hair white!"

I had never been so happy to see anyone in my entire life. Ellie held her hands up in the air and slumped against the cave wall.

"Why were you running?"

"The question should be, why are you in here and not where your mother told you to be!" Ellie came over and put her arm around my shoulders. "Why?"

"WILL SOMEONE TELL ME WHAT THE HELL IS GOING ON?" I yelled, losing my patience at the apparent deception that was underway. I then realized I had sworn in front of a child and slapped my hand over my mouth. "Sarah, come out, *koukla*."

"Ah, there you are!" Ellie let go of me and walked over to Sarah. Just as she was doing that, I heard more sounds of running, and I saw Stelios come to a stop. At least I didn't shoot at him, because if I had, I would have been dead. Stelios had served with my father and my uncle Petros at Skra and was the best marksman in all of Thessaly.

More running and a few more of the Resistance showed up. I looked around and saw familiar faces and some I didn't recognize. While I was busy trying to guess who was coming towards us, Ellie had taken off Sarah's shoes and wrapped her feet in torn cloth shreds. Someone I didn't know approached Ellie, and the child was handed over. Ellie gave me my shoes back.

"Can someone tell me what is going on?"

"I will, but you have to be patient," Ellie said to me before she turned to Stelios, and the two of them walked away. They talked briefly, and Ellie patted Stelios on the shoulder before he and the rest of the team left.

"This has turned into a strange day."

"Strange day for you, life-ending for some," Ellie said cryptically and pulled me towards her. "I think it's time we had a chat."

That was all she said as we made our way out of the cave. To my surprise, two Italian soldiers were lying dead at the mouth of the cave. They were being stripped of their guns and uniforms as we left.

"Can I ask about them?"

"You can, but I won't tell you until we get to the cabin."

We hadn't taken a few steps towards the cabin when a loud explosion came from the direction of the roadway followed by gunfire. I could see black smoke billowing in the wind.

"It's not your fight for now, Zoe. Let's get out of here quickly."

Ellie drew her gun and broke out into a run. I followed her and away from the gunfire and screams.

CHAPTER 21

Ellie set a good pace and I unenthusiastically ran right after her. The sun was going down and we wanted to be in the cabin before it set. I didn't think Ellie cared much for the curfew and I wanted to ask why we were running like headless chickens, but Ellie ignored my requests for a more leisurely pace. We arrived at the trail leading up to Athena's Bluff and I stopped at the start of the track. I turned to find that Ellie had gone further ahead and disappeared behind some trees. I thought that she must have forgotten where the path started. I didn't have the energy to go after her and assumed she would double back. I turned to walk up the narrow trail only to find myself being hauled back.

"What in God's name are you doing?!" I asked, irritated as yet another cousin had used my shirt as a leash.

"You're going the wrong way."

"I know my way up Athena's Bluff! It's this way," I replied and set off once again. I took two steps towards the trail before Ellie dragged me back.

"All right, Elisavet, you are making me angry! Stop doing that!"

Ellie laughed. "Has anyone ever told you that your hair gets redder when you're angry?"

"Are you drunk?"

Ellie looked at me with that enigmatic smile of hers. To my surprise, she took my hand and walked towards the brush instead of following the narrow trail. She went through the bushes and I decided not to follow her because I just didn't have the energy to cut my way through. I heard her laughing at me on the other side.

"Ellie, we need to be up at the cabin before curfew. Cutting through the bushes to get up there is crazy. We have a perfectly good track!"

"Trust me."

"Dear God, why do you want to make me crazy?"

"Stop praying to God and come through. You give up too easily, ZoZo. Have faith."

"It doesn't require faith to know we are going to be cutting and chopping our way up the mountain long into the night to get to the cabin."

I didn't have a machete and I knew Ellie didn't have one either. With a heavy sigh, I reasoned that if she wanted me to follow her, she must have a plan. She was always prepared, so I pushed through the thick scrub and joined her expecting to find the tools to make our journey up the mountain.

To my surprise, in front of me was a narrow path, clear of brush and with enough room for us to get through. It would be more difficult for Ellie, who wasn't skinny like me, but it was a path.

"I'm going to ask the obvious. Did you do this? Why did you do this when there is a perfectly good track?"

"I had to occupy my time while you had your beauty sleep." Ellie chuckled and put her hand on my back. "Okay, let's go!"

"That does not make sense."

"It will once we get to the cabin."

Ellie hunched over before she started walking. I was right behind her. "Did you use a machete?"

"Yes, it was difficult, but I was motivated."

"Why? Just tell me why?"

"Always think that the impossible is possible. That's how we will win this war."

"That still doesn't make any sense to me."

"By using whatever weapon we have to cut them down, like this bush. We will win."

That still didn't make any sense. What did the war have to do with the trail? I would find out soon enough.

We arrived at the cabin just as dusk settled over the valley. I stopped and marveled at the sight before me. It's a sight I had seen many times, but it still took my breath away. The valley was bathed in burnt orange.

As I marveled at the picturesque vista before me, I was acutely aware that I had run away from a battle. This was my home, my country, and I was hiding up a hill while my brothers and sisters were fighting down below. I wanted to be down there to fight with them. I wanted to try to make up for being a failure in the forest.

I looked over at the track and wondered if I could go down there and join in. Ellie must have read my mind because she took hold of my hand and pulled me towards the cabin.

"It's not your fight tonight."

I turned away and looked at her. "How do you know that was what I was thinking?"

Ellie smiled. "I know you, Zoe. I know your heart and that you want to be down there, in the battle, but it won't be tonight." She held up her hand to forestall my objections. "I know you have patience…"

I glowered. No one had ever accused me of being patient without making some other disparaging remark soon after.'

"Stop scowling. You claim you don't have patience. Everyone that knows you will say you don't, but I'm here to tell you that you do have patience."

"I'm here to tell you that you're drunk." I grumbled and walked toward the cabin. I had only taken a few steps when I noticed something that wasn't quite right. I backtracked and stood in front of the regular path leading up the mountain. It was different from the last time I had been here. I was sure of it. Athena's Bluff could not be reached by any other means other than up the narrow track or the hacked out track that Ellie had created. The Italians wouldn't know about the latter. Why had Ellie created the pathway through the brush? It was another mystery in a long day full of secrets.

I turned around when I heard Ellie's chuckle. "I've won a bet tonight," she said in a sing-song voice. "You just won me some money, ZoZo."

"I'd rather have food than money because we can't eat money."

"We can buy food if you know who to ask. Tell me what you see, even if it's dark."

"There's something wrong with the path."

"Well, yes, we already worked that out."

"We?" I looked up and pointed to myself.

"All right, you worked it out, but I knew you would. Now, tell me, what is different from the last time you were up here?"

"The rocks."

Ellie laughed and slapped her thigh. She *was* drunk, there was no doubt about it now. I couldn't smell any alcohol on her. It had to be some strange brew if it didn't stink.

"Oh, thank the Lord, you are incredible."

"It wasn't that hard to figure out."

"To you, it's not that hard because of your photographic memory. To other people, it would be a miracle that they could remember how the path looked the last time they were here."

"It's a good parlor trick. The rocks look different and appear to be fake." I took a step forward to go investigate the fake rocks, but I was quickly pulled back. "Stop that! It must be a family trait that you all yank my shirt or my hair!" I angrily said and gave Ellie my fiercest scowl. It didn't have any effect on her. She laughed.

"Did Stav pull your hair again?"

"That's not funny, Elisavet! I'm going to stab his foot if he does it again."

"Was he trying to get your attention?"

"He was a *malarka*!"

Ellie giggled and pulled me towards her. "I'm sorry I

pulled your shirt. By the way, it's not a simple trick you can do to amuse people. Your trick, as you call it, will save lives."

"You're funny when you're drunk."

"I'm not drunk." Ellie took my hand and led me to the edge of the path. She pulled me down, so we were both on our haunches. "See those pretty rocks?"

"They look fake."

"The path is booby-trapped."

"You booby-trapped a path up a mountain? Didn't you have anything else to do?"

"I had a lot to do, but I did have a good reason for cutting all that brush."

"Were you bored?"

"No. I used the cabin to protect some people before they were moved on to another location."

"That's why we went through the brush. I should have thought of that!"

"Why should *you* have thought of it?"

"I know; I'm a useless soldier."

"No, that isn't what I asked. Why do you think Athena's Bluff needs protection? Did you think the forest, the cabin, or the rocks need protection?"

"No."

"You only protect something worth protecting. As I said, I used the cabin last night to provide a secure place for some people. It was used to hide Allied soldiers."

"Oh, thank goodness, I thought I had had a bad dream and couldn't work out why I was dreaming about a man dressed as a woman. Barry makes one hell of an ugly woman."

"He makes an ugly woman, but as a man, he is very handsome." Ellie laughed as she led me back to the cabin.

"Didn't think he was *that* handsome. Angelos is cuter."

Ellie didn't say anything for a moment and when I looked up at her, she was staring out towards the mountains. "Were you smitten with Barry?" I asked, knowing it was silly.

"No, my heart belongs to one man."

"That's going to make me throw up," I joked, and it got the desired result in making Ellie smile.

"One thing to remember, Zo. If you decide to throw up or if you have to go out in the night to relieve yourself, try not to stray onto the path. You're going to blow yourself up."

"It will be raining shit."

Ellie burst out laughing. We both laughed uncontrollably for a few minutes.

It felt good to laugh, and for a moment I forgot we were in a war. Our hilarity came to an end when a loud explosion was heard from outside the cabin. We looked at each other before Ellie drew her weapon and pushed me behind the door.

I realized I had made a colossal mistake once again. My crossbow was sitting on a boulder on the lookout. Whoever was outside and had triggered the explosion was either dead or was going to die. I had had enough of being so inept. I tried to follow Ellie out of the cabin, but she stopped me.

"Do you remember I said you had patience?"

"Yes."

"Good. Find where you put it and wear it now." Ellie

turned and left the cabin. I was going to ignore her, but moments later, she popped her head back inside.

"Well, you know how you wanted food more than money?"

"Yes."

"The Lord heard you." Ellie's arm snaked out, and half a rabbit, still dripping with blood, appeared. "I hate skinning rabbits. Would you like to?"

It was absurd. Ellie was holding a rabbit by its ears. Its bottom half had ended up down the mountain someplace, and the other half had hit one of the beams of the porch.

"How is it possible that you can't cook?"

"I can cook; I just don't like skinning animals."

"Is it against your religion?" I asked not knowing what her religion said about rabbits or if they were sacred or something like that.

Ellie stared me at me and then at the rabbit. "No, it's not against my religion to skin a rabbit. I just don't like it."

I chuckled. "Arty didn't like hunting, and you don't like skinning a rabbit. Are we related?"

"You have such a smart mouth," Ellie teased. "Can *you* cook this rabbit so we can eat it?"

"Hand over Mister Rabbit."

Ellie gave a lopsided grin. "How do you know it's a 'he'?" she said and waved her hand under the missing rabbit's bottom half.

"He won't care," I replied and took hold of the rabbit's ears. "We have some rods Papa used for the Easter spit where the firewood is kept dry." I got up and opened the door wider. I was expecting to find a blood-soaked porch timber floor, but that was not the case. There was some blood, but nothing that needed the entire boards scrubbed back. "At least the rabbit didn't make much of a nuisance of himself by dripping blood everywhere."

"I'm certain he is honored you think he was respectful of your porch when he died. Can you please cook him so we can eat?"

"We're going to have a wonderful dinner."

CHAPTER 22

Cooking the rabbit on the spit brought back memories of happier days. The smell conjured up one of my favorite memories of being with my family. The last time we had all come up to Athena's Bluff was to 'inspect' Thieri's carpentry, and we piled on some good-natured teasing about his work and about the girl he wanted to marry. Late in the afternoon, we enjoyed a feast of lamb on the spit cooked by my father, and roasted vegetables, goat's cheese, and oh, those magnificent olives I loved so much. My papa wasn't much of a cook, but when it came to roasting meat, he was the best in all of Farsala. This was true because I drew a trophy for his cooking and gave it to him. How I yearned to be there again and have all of this death and misery be just a bad dream... Every day I longed to wake up from this nightmare.

Ellie must have noticed my mood, and she threw some of the rabbit meat at me to dislodge me from my wallowing. Not one to let good food go to waste, I plucked it out of the air and ate it. We had the rabbit on a makeshift spit, and it was better than I thought it was going to be. We had some stale bread that we toasted and hoped it wasn't going to make us sick. At least it was warm. The old figs were too dry and we chose not to eat them. I wasn't ready to die from fig poisoning. The meal may have been entirely forgettable, but my papa used to say it's not the food that makes a good meal but the people around the table. We didn't talk because we were too busy eating like the starving Greeks we were. I hadn't eaten anything for most of the day, and by the time the rabbit was ready, I was famished.

"You were wallowing."

I chewed on the bread and simply nodded. "The last time we came up here, Thieri told us he was going to ask Melina to marry him just as soon as he finished with the porch. He wanted to bring her out here and do that romantic thing men do."

"You mean to get down on one knee and propose?"

I nodded. "The woman knows what he's going to say or else she's not very bright."

"I thought you were a romantic. You read enough romance novels to know that's what men do."

"I *am* a romantic, but I want the man I marry to sweep me off my feet and offer me more than just a ring." I flung my arms in the air to signify the world or something equally silly.

"It doesn't work that way."

"It should," I replied with a shrug. What did I know about love? Nothing, but I wanted more than a man on bended knee and a tiny ring. Honestly, I didn't care about rings or other jewelry. Most girls my age loved all of that nonsense, but I didn't.

"Melina would have loved the grand gesture of a new home. She was a lucky girl."

"Not so lucky," I replied quietly. "Melina died in the earthquake."

There wasn't much to be said about that, so we sat there in silence. Ellie rested against the cabin wall. There was a full moon, and Athena's Bluff was bathed in bright moonlight. I sat on the log and looked out towards Mount Ossa, my sketchbook beside me in readiness for when I would find some time before bedtime to draw.

I had made it a nightly habit to draw before bedtime. For years I told everyone who would listen (and those that didn't want to hear) that one day I would go to the Athens Art Academy just like my mother. I wanted to be just like her and have the opportunities she had.

The distinctive smell of cigarette smoke made me turn around in time to see Ellie take a drag of her cigarette. Memories of happier days came flooding back again and I had to choke back the tears that threatened to overwhelm me. Ellie must have read my mind because she sniffed the air and smirked, which caused me to giggle.

"When did you start smoking?"

"They say when you get married, you pick up the bad habits of your spouse. You can blame Angel for this."

"It smells better than the ones Papa used to smoke." I could still remember the foul-smelling smoke that would waft through the house. I would have rejoiced if that smell would once again seep through our home.

"Your Papa smoked cigars. Want to know why these are better?"

"I'm afraid to ask."

"They're not made of dung."

Ellie winked at me. We burst out laughing at the memory that had become legendary in our family. In my defense, all I could say was that it hadn't been just my idea. My 'dung' cigarettes had become infamous not only to my immediate family but the hilarious story had spread to the entire village. They never let me forget my smoking experiment.

Arty and I thought it would be a great idea to roll our own just like our fathers did. We didn't know it was going to be that hard because we had studied how they did it. Since I had an excellent recall, we did the same. The only thing we didn't have was tobacco, and it wasn't because we couldn't get it—Uncle Petros grew it, but his tobacco crop wasn't ready to harvest. I tried to steal some from my older brother, Michael, but I ended up getting smacked on the backside for my troubles. It was a case of 'if at first you don't succeed, then you improvise.'

I found another way. We used cow dung instead of tobacco.

We were having one of our enormous family gatherings, and while the rest of the family were dancing and ignoring us, Arty and I snuck into the barn with cow dung in hand, so to speak, and rolled our cigarettes. We were so proud of ourselves, and we were going to be as sophisticated as the women we saw at the cinema. We tried it and found that we couldn't stop choking from the awful taste and smell. Setting fire to dung does not create a pleasant aroma and I was in such a hurry to get rid of the foul odor that I threw the cigarette over my shoulder. To my dismay, it landed onto bales of hay. We panicked after we saw the smoke emanating from the stack. I grabbed what I thought was water and threw it on the fire in the hope of extinguishing it before my father and uncles came running. Unfortunately, it wasn't water but lamp oil. The hay exploded and we had a significant fire in the barn. We raced outside as if our backsides were on fire and screamed for help. At the time, it was embarrassing to have set the barn ablaze, but even more so when we had to explain how the hay bales had caught on fire. It became a joke recreated exuberantly and often embellished by my brothers.

I couldn't stop laughing. Just when I thought it would peter out, one look at Ellie taking a drag of her cigarette would set me off again.

"It was Arty's idea. I just went along with it."

Ellie giggled. "I have never believed that story, ZoZo. That had your fingerprints all over it. Cow dung in a cigarette is a genius idea for cows who wanted to smoke!"

"I may have had something to do with coming up with the smoking idea but it was Arty's idea to replace the tobacco with dung!" I chuckled and then looked out at the moonlit vista before me on thinking about the hilarious escapade that my cousin and I got into.

"You have good memories to remember my darling sister. She loved you so much."

"I failed her."

Ellie didn't say anything for a long moment. Cigarette smoke drifted across to me, and I knew I was right. I had failed Arty, and Ellie blamed me for getting her sister killed.

"I could tell you to stop blaming yourself," Ellie finally said, "but you won't listen because, in your heart, you feel you were responsible."

I didn't have anything to say because Ellie was right.

"Do you know what you can do with the disappointment and anger you are feeling?" Ellie leaned forward and tapped me on the knee. "You can fight and save someone who may not survive if it weren't for you."

"That doesn't bring Arty back."

"No, neither does sitting here feeling like a failure. You think you failed. So, what do you do with that? Does it consume you? Do you sit on a mountain and waste the precious time the Lord has given you on something you can't change? Now what?"

"I'm useless, Ellie. I can't fight or run fast enough. I couldn't protect Arty. I tried to save another girl, a Jewess. She was running around in a forest, hunted like an animal by the Italians and Germans. She died because I was useless. That evening you rescued me? I was trying to save a man from getting shot near the grove. All I managed to do was get the man killed, and then, to add to my failures, I got smacked in the head by a tree."

"That's a lot of failures."

I nodded. "I know."

"You're wrong. You can't see the one thing that stands out from that list that you call

'failures.' It's not what happened to those people, or what happened to Arty, but how you acted. You tried, Zoe. Many do nothing, but you tried."

"They are all still dead."

"Yes, they are. I hope that...I wish that everyone we love would never die, but an earthquake can take our loved ones in a matter of seconds, a bombing can shatter our hearts and..." Ellie stopped midsentence and took a breath. "It's not that they died, but what we did to try to save them."

"What use is it to try and not succeed?"

"Oh, Zoe." Ellie patted the side of the bench for me to sit. I joined her, and she put her arm around me. "When you try, you are giving the most precious thing in the world to them. You are giving a part of you. Not everything will go your way. It probably won't, but you still have to try."

"Trying isn't good enough. I don't know how to fight."

"Do you think every Greek knows how to fight?"

"No, but I want to be just like you. I want to fight to protect the people I love and protect the ones that I don't know because it's the right thing to do."

Ellie closed her eyes and sighed. "Ah, my darling Zoe, it is only with people like you that we will prevail." She offered me a cigarette, but since I had sworn off them for the rest of my life, I passed on the opportunity. She was a worldly woman and someone I longed to imitate, but she was everything I wasn't—tall, confident, and courageous. I was certain Ellie never failed at anything she did.

"You won't be able to go up against trained soldiers. You're too small and inexperienced. You must use your brain and outwit them. You have to use the gifts the Lord has given you."

"I think at this point, being a wife is my only option if I manage to survive the war."

Ellie chuckled. "You will never be *just* a wife. You were not born to be 'just a wife.' You're going to make someone the luckiest man alive, but I think he won't be able to handle you."

It was fortunate that I wasn't drinking my wine because I would have choked on it. Ellie had a smile on her face that reached her eyes. I loved her dearly, but she did enjoy teasing me.

"Arty told me about Apostolos being sweet on you."

"He's Athenian."

"Isn't it good that he's from Athens? You're going to go there and study and be his wife."

I laughed at the idea that Apostolos was the man I would marry. "I would rather eat dirt. Apostolos may be a nice boy, but I don't want to be his wife."

"And those eyes! You hate blue eyes."

"They are unnaturally blue."

Ellie brought her cup up to her lips and sipped on the liquid. "Angel's eyes are blue."

"Angel has beautiful dark blue eyes. That's different."

"You are going to be a handful… The poor man."

We looked at each other and smiled. The mention of Ellie's husband allowed me to ask the question about Angelos I had wanted to ask since Ellie rescued me in the forest.

"Where is Angel?" I poured myself some wine and filled Ellie's cup.

"Ah, that question," Ellie said and went on to drink from her cup. She just stared at the cup for a long moment. To my surprise, she then got up, took my plate, and went inside.

CHAPTER 23

I hadn't expected Ellie to disappear on me. If I had been more observant and not obsessing over my faults and obvious idiotic decisions, I would have seen there was something wrong.

I sat on the boulder and looked out across the valley that was cast in shadows and decided that my mother was right. I had wallowed in my grief for too long, and it was time to stop. I was in two minds about getting up and going inside to talk to Ellie or being patient and allowing her the time she needed.

I glanced at the closed door behind me and decided that I needed to be patient; as foreign as that was to me, this time, it was the only course of action. I picked up my sketchbook and took out my pencil. My mind was not on drawing, but I had to do something with my hands. My pencil hovered over the paper and I started to draw while my thoughts were on the love that Ellie and Angel shared.

Ellie and Angelos were always together. Not that she didn't want to be with her husband all the time, but they still acted as if they were happy to be in each other's company. I've seen the marriage of my uncle Yiannis and his wife, and it was exhausting. Yiannis was a curmudgeon (even in his early forties!). He was always correcting his wife or claiming to be better at something than she was. By the time I'd leave their home, I was ready to take a brick and throw it at him. That's not a marriage; that's torture.

In comparison, Ellie and Angelos were best friends and then marriage mates. It was sweet and, in my opinion, one of the beautiful things about their marriage. Angel was attentive and always supported Ellie in whatever she wanted to do. My parents were also like that, and it gave me hope that one day I would find someone to share my life with, someone who loved me and whom I would love back with equal measure, someone I could be there to support in their dreams.

I was too shy (a trait I rarely suffered from) to ask Mama or Ellie when they found out that the man they married was 'the one.' How did you know? The romantic novels I read were unrealistic, but surely it wasn't fireworks or the color of their eyes that made them desirable. There had to be more to it than that. How did someone get to the 'heavy-like' stage or even the 'falling off the cliff' stage? I wouldn't have to worry about that because, in war, you didn't have time to fall in love.

I heard the door open, but I didn't look around. Ellie would choose to talk to me or not. I was going to make it easy on her rather than blast my way through.

"Zoe," Ellie softly called my name, and I turned towards her. "What are you drawing?"

"Flowers." I held up the sketchbook to reveal the line art. It required no skill, and it allowed me to think.

"Do you know why I love you? You have the unique ability to be patient without making it obvious that you are patient."

"I still think you're drunk."

"It takes skill to appear to be concentrating when you're thinking of several things at the same time."

"Drawing flowers is not something that requires a lot of thought."

"I'm sorry I was abrupt with you; I didn't intend to be so rude."

"It's all right," I replied and went back to my flowers. I was content not to push.

Silence descended once again between us, and I continued to draw. The occasional sound of gunfire was heard somewhere in the valley and that was something I didn't want to dwell on. Someone had just lost their life in that endless round of bloodletting.

"Can you stop drawing?" I put my sketchbook aside and turned towards Ellie.

She had taken a blanket and draped it around herself. Under her arm was another blanket. She gave it to me so I could wrap myself in its warm embrace. Ellie brought a chair with her and sat beside me.

"You have the patience of a saint."

I burst out laughing, equally for her delivery and her humor. I had no patience and we both knew it. She reached over and tapped my knee. "You are a loyal sister to me. It's time for you to know the truth."

"You don't have to tell me if you don't want to."

"I was always going to tell you, but I didn't know when it would be the right time to do so."

"Where is Angel?" I asked again, and this time I brought my makeshift seat closer to her. "Has he done something stupid and that's why he's not with you? I've heard men do stupid things all the time; they can't help it."

Ellie didn't react to my attempt at humor, and that's how I knew this was serious.

"I'm ready to talk to you about why you are up here."

"All right."

Ellie had also brought out another bottle of wine she had found in the woodshed. Thieri had a distillery, and there was a lot of wine he had been storing for his engagement and wedding. If we ran out of water to drink, we could end up killing ourselves drinking retsina.

Ellie held up the two mugs and poured me a drink before she did the same for herself. She took a sip from the cup and made a face before she took a deep breath. "For me to answer your question about where Angel is, I have to tell you what happened."

I didn't want to interrupt, so I kept my mouth shut.

"We knew the Germans were coming; that wasn't a secret. We didn't know when they would get to us. I joined Angel and the other boys, and we prepared for battle in Thessaloniki."

"You were going to fight?"

"With everything I had. I wasn't going to let Angel face the enemy on his own without me. We are Spartans, and we never run from a fight. Unfortunately, the Germans broke through and we had to fall back to Panteleimonas, where we kept on fighting with our Allies."

"The Allies were doing a lot of retreating."

"They had to, or they would have been killed or captured."

"I would stake my life that Angel did not run away from the fight."

"You are right. My Angel would never run like a coward. He was with a small band of soldiers that fell back so they could get the reinforcements we were promised. They didn't surrender and kept on fighting. They had help from the surrounding villages. I had never been in battle before, Zoe, and nothing can prepare you for it. The Germans were like a pack of wild dogs and unstoppable."

"Were you scared?"

"Terrified, but we had a job to do. The Germans were too strong. We fell back to Mount Olympus, but they kept on coming."

"Was Angel killed in battle?"

"No." Ellie took a sip. "That would have been better for him." Her voice broke with emotion.

"Getting killed in battle is never a better option."

Ellie shook her head. I should have censored myself, but I couldn't do that with my favorite cousin. I had always been honest and direct with her. However, my words had hurt her, and I shouldn't have been so blunt.

"Angel wanted to fight until the end. He told the women to run to Larissa to get help from the British."

"How did he get word that the British were still in Larissa? By carrier pigeon?"

Ellie wiped her eyes with the back of her sleeve. "He didn't get any word from the British that it was safe in Larissa. Angel told me to leave and lead the women to safety. He was my commanding officer, and I had to obey. Just before I led the women away, he told me the truth."

"He lied to get the women away, didn't he?"

"Yes. I didn't want to leave. I wanted to fight and die with my Angel, but if I didn't follow orders, the women and children with us would also die."

"It's the 'no secrets rule.' Couldn't Angel have spared you the pain of knowing what was going to happen?"

"No, not even then. When you get married and the love of your life is honest with you, you trust him with your life. We didn't keep secrets."

"He truly lived up to his name."

"Angel by name, angel by character. Angelos was the most courageous man I have ever met. I left him to fight the beasts alone with his brothers." Ellie took a deep breath before she brought the wine bottle up to her lips, forgoing the cup, and drank from it.

I didn't know what to say, so I kept quiet while Ellie drank. She wiped her mouth with the back of her hand and gazed at me. "One day you will love a man who would willingly give his life for yours. That kind of man is rare in this world."

"I will be lucky if that happens to me."

"You will find a man like Angel and your father. There is a man out there that is just for you who will be just like my Angel."

Ellie's words were slurring just a little. If she wanted to

finish off the bottle of retsina, I wasn't going to stop her. She had every right to get drunk.

"So, Angel didn't die in battle?"

"No. When the Germans captured them, they ended up being transferred to a POW camp with other Allied soldiers."

"Did they know..."

Ellie looked away and shook her head. "Not at the time. I found out he was still alive, and I was desperate to find out where they had sent him."

"Were you going to rescue him?"

Ellie smiled and patted me on the head. "You would have roused up a small army, right?"

"In record time. Nothing would have stopped me."

"Life isn't like one of your books, Zoe. I did rouse up a Mavrakis army, and I found out that he was in the POW camp in Thessaloniki, so I rushed there."

"How did you know where to go once you reached Thessaloniki?"

"It was the strangest thing. All I knew was that Angel was in Thessaloniki, and I was trying to evade the Germans because I had no identity papers. I was looking for a man who I was told could help me, but as I wandered into the street to meet him, you wouldn't guess who I literally ran into. It was Stella!"

"Our Aunty Stella?"

"The one and only. Stella had a young man with her. He was tall, blonde, with the bluest eyes..."

"I bet he was from Athens," I joked, knowing it would get a laugh out of Ellie. I could laugh at myself for my silliness sometimes and this time I was using it to my advantage.

Ellie pulled me to her. She affectionately kissed the top of my head. "I didn't ask him. I think Aunty Stella has got herself a younger man."

It was my turn to stare slack-jawed at my cousin. "You're joking."

"I am, and I love the look on your face." Ellie giggled and sat back in her seat. "Paul was one of Angel's friends, but I didn't recognize him at first."

"Did they know where Angel was located?"

"Yes, he was being kept at the Pavlos Melas camp."

"Ooh, one of our heroes! Pavlos Melas was a war hero who fought to free Macedonia from the Turks, but he died in battle."

"Your love of history is astonishing."

"I remember our war heroes. How did they know where he was?"

"I don't know and didn't care how they knew. All I wanted was to see my Angel. To my delight, the Germans allowed the villagers to bring food to them. Aunty Stella and I visited him just one time. I brought him some food and stayed with him until we had to leave."

"You never went back? They didn't allow you to see him again?"

Ellie's face crumpled as the tears flowed down her cheeks. The tears said all that needed to be said. I reached out and hugged her to me. The loss of Angelos robbed her of the man that she loved more than herself. I was eleven years old when Ellie told me she was getting married to a young man from Thessaloniki. Ellie was seventeen and didn't need to bother with an eleven-year-old cousin, but she came over to where I was drawing by the river. She told me all about Angelos, and he also came down to meet me. I felt special that they would do that just for me. When Ellie sat back and wiped her eyes, I wanted to know what had happened to Angel in the camp, but I chose to stay quiet.

CHAPTER 24

Ellie sat with her back leaning against the cabin wall and her eyes closed. "You're getting better at the patience game."

"No, I'm not."

She opened her eyes and looked out over the moonlit horizon. I couldn't take it anymore.

"What happened?"

"Let's not talk about it tonight."

"All right," I replied, and after a beat, I said, "Did you sit shiva?"

Ellie looked at me, and I wondered if I had said the wrong thing. Maybe she didn't perform the Jewish mourning prayer. "I'm sorry, Ellie. I had forgotten you don't worship the Jewish God."

"The Jewish God and the Christian God are the same."

"I thought you believed in the Goddess, like Aunty Stella."

Ellie's smile reached her eyes for the first time since she

had started talking about Angelos. "I do that to appease the parts of our family that think I have betrayed my Orthodox faith."

"That doesn't make sense."

"No, bigotry and stupidity never make sense. The family is used to Aunty Stella's belief in a Goddess and her pagan faith, if you can call it that. They think it's harmless. God is not female, so they are amused rather than angry."

"Is Aunty Stella a Jew as well?"

Ellie laughed. "My goodness, the thought of Stella being Jewish would be more than the Rabbi could handle. No, she's not Jewish. Aunty Stella is a real pagan. She believes there are many Gods and Goddesses, like in Ancient Greece."

"Ooh, she believes that Artemis is real?"

"Yes, she does. The supreme god is a woman and she worships the Goddess. I only pretend to be a pagan so I can appease some in the family."

"No wonder they call her crazy Stella."

"I don't think that's the reason, but Stella likes the nickname. She told me that if I wanted the fanatical members of the family—"

"Yiannis, Dion, the coward, and Grandfather Dimitri are the ones that come to mind."

"Yes, they were the ones more comfortable with me being a pagan than a Jew. I chose to make them believe the less evil choice and that was being a pagan. My parents and my brothers knew why I reverted to Judaism and accepted it."

"Can I ask you a question? Why is it that Uncle Dion

and the others don't have a problem with Stella being a pagan, but they have a problem with you being Jewish?"

"The answer to that question is steeped in history, bigotry, and hate. The Jews have been despised everywhere they settle. They need a country of their own, and I think that place is our spiritual home—the promised land."

"Home? You were born in Larissa and this is your home."

Ellie poured herself some more wine. I declined because I wanted to discover the answer to my question. I couldn't do that if I had more than one cup of wine.

"Home is not the place where you are born. Home is the place that makes your heart sing. Where is home for you?"

Where was home to me? Where did I want to go more than anywhere else? That was an easy question to answer. I wanted to follow in my mother's footsteps and go to Athens. To study art and be like her. My mother was my inspiration. Then I wanted to travel and see the world.

"Athens."

Ellie smiled knowingly. "For all your talk about Athenians and your dislike for them, you still want to go to Athens?"

"Don't make fun of me." Of course, Ellie was right. I hadn't been shy about voicing my opinion on Athenians. "Sparta doesn't have an art school."

"No, it doesn't," Ellie replied with a smile. "I'm going to presume that Ancient Sparta didn't have one either—not much use for it while they were training to fight."

"Why did you ask if you already knew the answer?"

"I wanted to see if that was still your dream. We all have dreams, Zoe. You've been talking about going to

Athens and studying at the best Art Academy for a long time. Your heart knows what it wants."

"Where does your heart say it wants to go?"

"For as long as I could remember, I wanted to visit the Holy Land, the land God promised my ancestors, the Promised Land. When the war is over, that is where my heart will lead me."

"Your ancestors are Greek, and you're not Jewish..." I stopped when I noticed Ellie's sly smile. "Oh wait...did you say you went back to Judaism? Don't you mean 'converted' to Judaism?"

"That took you longer than I thought. Does your head still hurt?"

"It aches a little, but let's get back to your conversion."

"It wasn't a conversion. My maternal grandmother was a Jewess from Thessaloniki."

"I know Grandmother Elisavet came from Thessaloniki, but you are wrong about her being Jewish. She was Michael's godmother. Only Christians are allowed to be godparents."

"Yiayia Elisavet converted to Christianity when she married Pappou Stavros. Being Jewish is not washed away when someone converts to another faith. I've always been Jewish, so have all my brothers and my mother."

"How do you become Jewish?"

"You are Jewish if your mother is Jewish. It comes from the maternal line."

I was surprised that I didn't know the family history. How was it possible? "Are you sure?" I hope that didn't sound as stupid as I thought it did. I looked up at Ellie, who was smiling.

"Yes, I'm sure. How do you feel about the news I'm Jewish and not pagan?"

That had to be the strangest question anyone had asked me. I was more annoyed by something else entirely, which I didn't want to give voice to. "I don't care."

"Yes, you do. You were surprised that I was not a pagan. I could see it in your eyes."

I sighed. "It's not that you are Jewish. It's because you *are* Jewish."

"Can you explain that to me?"

"I kept sending you drawings of a Goddess in the woods, and you didn't say that it was wrong in your religion to worship a Goddess! I know it's forbidden because Father Haralambos told us about the Ten Commandments."

"You shall have no other gods before Me."

"That's not the bad part. You shall not make idols is the second one, and I was sending you idols to worship! I drew all sorts of pagan symbols! I was drawing something detestable in your religion!" The look on Ellie's face showed that my voice and hands were being a little too overly dramatic, and I was quite sure even the Italians in the valley could hear me.

Ellie stood up and pulled me towards her. "I love you, Zoe Lambros! You are unique in this world, my sister." She almost lifted me off the ground. "I adore you for being you."

"Who else would I be?"

Ellie laughed and shook her head in apparent amazement that I was me. It made me smile, but I was still worried about the drawings I had sent her.

"What did you do with the drawings?"

"I kept the ones of the animals, but those of the Goddess I gave to Stella." Ellie reached into her satchel, and I was expecting her to take out one of the drawings of the animals. She unfolded a paper. It was one of mine because I had written ZL on the back in the corner.

Ellie stared at the paper for a long time before she gave it to me. I took it, and my heart leaped a little. Staring back at me was Angel's smiling face. His blonde curly hair and beautiful dark blue eyes. His eyes crinkled on the edges, and the smile was genuine. I adored him because he loved my favorite cousin and was a good man. I felt an overwhelming need to cry, but I didn't want to make Ellie upset as well.

"I keep that with me always. It's the only picture I have of my Angelos."

"I can draw you some more. I will do one tonight."

"We need to sleep…"

"It won't take me long, and I know the perfect picture to draw. I remember stuff, Ellie."

Ellie chuckled and nodded. "You certainly have been blessed, ZoZo. I will go inside and prepare our beds." She got up from her log and kissed me on the forehead before she went inside the cabin.

"Ellie, why did Mama not want me to be at the farm today?"

Ellie stopped. She didn't turn around for a few moments. When she did, she had an odd expression on her face that I couldn't decipher. "'For it is not an enemy who taunts me— then I could bear it; it is not an adversary who deals insolently with me— then I could hide from him. But it is you, a man, my equal, my companion, my familiar friend.'"

"What?"

"It's from Psalms. David is talking about being betrayed by a friend."

"I don't understand, which friend was betrayed?"

Ellie leaned against the door and sighed deeply. "I don't think…"

I put my sketchbook down and stood up. "Why don't you want to tell me?"

After a long beat, Ellie came back outside and sat down. She motioned for me to sit and I reluctantly sat down. "This is just an example. What would you do if Stavros betrayed me?"

"I would kill him."

"Would you? He's your cousin, as close to you as a brother."

"You are my sister; we are blood. He would cease to be family. He would cease to be anything other than Judas worthy of death. I know you said it as an example but did Stav do something stupid??"

"No! You must listen carefully when I'm talking to you. You get angry and then your brain shuts off. Anger replaces your common sense." I felt once again miserable. "I can say that to you because you are my beloved cousin and sister. You must listen when people are speaking to you and not get so caught up in your anger."

"I'm confused. Who are we talking about? It's not Stav…" I stopped talking and realized who we were actually talking about. Someone had betrayed Angel and I felt tightness in my chest. "Who betrayed Angel?"

"One of our family, Zoe. We have a collaborator in our family and that betrayal cost Angel his life. The Germans executed my Angel." Ellie said, her voice barely above a whisper.

I sat there in stunned silence; nothing else mattered at that moment. Who had betrayed Angel? Why? I couldn't believe it. I opened my mouth to ask but I couldn't speak. Betrayal is death in my eyes. If I understood what Ellie was insinuating, then one of our family had betrayed Angel. One of us; a trusted family member had collaborated with the enemy.

"Who did this evil thing?" I finally managed to say. "They were one of us, in our family. Who did it? I knew something was odd back at the house. Everyone was acting strange. Your father, Uncle Ignatius, Uncle Yiannis, and all the aunties were there as well.

"What do you mean they were acting odd?"

"Before I left, Mama and Uncle Petros behaved like I dreamed about you rescuing me. Uncle Ignatius claimed he didn't know someone he once brought to the house to protect...it was just strange."

"Nothing escapes your notice, does it?"

"Well, this didn't require a lot of figuring out. It's not every day I find out that your beloved has been betrayed by family. How did you want me to respond? Sit here and not be enraged? Do you want me to knit while you tell me these things?" I shouldn't have been angry with Ellie, but the only response to betrayal is anger and then vengeance.

"Zoe, I love you dearly for being so passionate, devoted, and a fierce warrior for all that is right, but you have to learn to control that anger."

"I don't want to right now, if you don't mind."

Ellie nodded. "I understand, but when you find out who it is, I fear your anger will consume you and you will do something…."

"I will kill them. What else is there to do? Hang them from the nearest tree and let the vultures eat them. That's what I would do. Who did this treacherous thing? Who did this despicable crime?"

Ellie gazed out into the mountains. "You know who it is already."

"I don't know who it is. If I did, I would have killed him already."

"Why are you so sure it's a man and not a woman?"

"Only a man would be so treacherous."

"There are women who are just as evil as men but you are right. It was a man. Yiannis." Ellie's voice broke, and all I could do was stare at her dumbfounded by the revelation. Our uncle was the collaborator — blood betraying blood. I stood up because I couldn't stay seated. I needed to get up and do something with my hands. I needed to pace. "Yiannis, that spineless pig, betrayed your Angel? He was already a POW…what was left to betray? The Germans knew he was a soldier. No big surprise there."

"It's not the Greek part of him that the Germans cared about."

"I stood stock still and closed my eyes. "It was the Jewish part."

"Angelos didn't look like a Jew, and the Germans didn't suspect him. He was just another soldier. Someone went to the Germans and told them that Angel was a Jew. That someone was at the house this morning. He might as well have been the one who pulled the trigger and executed my Angel because that is what he did by telling the Germans."

In my opinion, the penalty for betrayal is death. No matter who it is. I turned away from Ellie and strode quickly to the boulder and picked up my crossbow. I hadn't taken two steps towards the path when Ellie took hold of me and lifted me off the ground.

"Let me go!" I screamed at her and tried to get out of the tight grip she had on me.

"No! You are not going back to the farm."

"I'm going to execute Judas myself." I was incensed. Angel did so much to help Yiannis, especially when he fell off his roof and needed help around the farm. Both Ellie and Angel were there helping him and his wife. That despicable pig. "Let me go!"

Ellie was a strong woman, much stronger than I was, and she dragged me into the cabin and slammed the door shut. She barred the door with her body and folded her arms. "This is NOT your fight."

"STOP SAYING THAT! You keep saying, 'it's not your fight,' but when will it be my fight? When *do* I stand up and fight?"

"I will tell you tomorrow. You will have a mission, Zoe, and it will be important. Do you believe me?"

"I want to believe you."

"Have I ever lied to you?"

"No."

"I'm not lying to you now. What is going on at the farm is not your concern. Yes, you are enraged by this betrayal. I know how much you loved Angelos, and he loved you too.

I know what honor, respect, and family mean to you. Have you taken the time to ask why *I'm* not at the farm?"

"I was getting to that. Why aren't you there? If it were me, I would have killed Yiannis the moment I found out. Dead."

"My father told me to leave the farm and come here. I wanted to be there and be the one to execute the bastard who betrayed my Angel, but I had been given an assignment. Good soldiers follow orders. My father is the head of what's left of our family, and his word is the law."

"That is wrong. You should be the one to shoot the traitor."

"Following orders is never easy, even when all you want to do is to disobey them."

"Is your assignment to babysit the infant?"

Ellie pushed herself off the door and came up to me. "You are not an infant. My presence here is not for *you* but for *me*. What my father did was to protect *me*. I have been consumed with grief over my Angel and there is NOTHING I can do to bring him back. My father, as I told you, is going to deal with his brother."

"Why am I here and not down there? I'm part of this family."

"You are here for me. My father wanted you to be with me because you are my sister. Someone that my father trusts to be with me and who understands the grief I am going through." Ellie cupped my face. "Do you understand?"

"I do."

"I want you to calm down and be my rock. If you fall apart, so will I."

"I will be Mount Olympus for you," I said seriously and meant every word. Being compared with the highest mountain in Greece made Ellie's face crease into a smile even though she was wiping the tears that tracked down her cheeks.

"I was hoping for a rock, but I'll take a whole mountain." Ellie put her arm around me and hugged me. "You are my rock, Zoe. I want you to focus…"

"Oh, I'm focused."

"No, you're not. You're coming up with three plans— how to get past me, how you will evade the patrols to get to the farm, and how to fulfill your duty as my sister and show support. You must obey the head of the family, and what's more, you are a soldier. You must follow orders."

"What if I don't want to follow those orders?"

"If your father was here, would you obey him? Even if those orders went against something you wanted to do?"

"Yes."

"My father is the head of our family. We must not forget our family's Spartan code. We must always remember what is important even when others don't."

"But…"

Ellie put her hand on my shoulder. "My father will never take your father's place in your heart, but he is your head, Zoe. He told me to leave the farm and leave it to him to mete out justice. I obeyed those orders. Do you understand?"

"I do, but…"

"What would your heroine Laskarina do?"

I took a deep breath and found myself trying to figure

out if I could outrun Ellie, but her eyes never left me. "Laskarina would follow orders."

"Are you better than Laskarina?"

"No."

"Will you please follow orders and not try to get past me? Promise me you will listen to me."

"You have my word."

"Good. We have a lot to discuss tomorrow. Let's go to bed."

"No. I want to go outside and draw. I'm too angry to sleep."

Ellie kissed me on the head. "Goodnight, and don't sleep outside."

I nodded and made my way out of the cabin. I looked back and wondered how Ellie coped with the realization her uncle had betrayed the man she loved. A gentle breeze rustled the trees and flipped open my sketchbook. I wasn't going to create just one drawing. I was going to draw so many Ellie would need a whole satchel to hold them.

CHAPTER 25

I was looking up at the ceiling above my bed, trying to form patterns to calm my mind. I was getting annoyed by the tree branch that was sliding back and forth against the cabin wall and the wind that howled outside. I hadn't slept well—my mind was on the traitorous pig and the evil he had perpetrated. I vowed I would never utter that despicable bastard's name again. The previous night my art reflected my mood, and I threw away the pieces that I had drawn of the traitor with his head cut off. Accidentally, I also threw away my favorite pencil, much to my disgust. I can't do my best work when I'm angry, and I certainly can't do it without my favorite pencil. I eventually focused enough to draw my favorite memory of Angelos and Ellie on their wedding day using the other pencil in my pack. It's a cruel God that rips apart that kind of love, a brutal, angry God that I had come to despise yet again.

Ellie's faith in God was still alive. I didn't understand how or why. The Jewish God is different from the Christian

God. While I was muttering to myself and throwing things, Ellie had been up and waited until I came inside so she could sleep. When I finally entered the cabin, I found that Ellie had given me the bed. She had set a flokati rug for herself on the floor. Once we were both settled, Ellie bolted the door shut. Her gun lay near her head, and if required, she would be ready. Not that anyone would be walking up the path in the middle of the night, and if they did, they would be blown asunder.

I closed my eyes, but I couldn't sleep. Ellie started to pray, and I wondered why she bothered. I didn't ask her.

The morning was the same, and nothing had changed overnight. Another day of this horrific war. What horrors would it bring? Would we be alive to see the sunset? I never used to be so melancholy, but the longer this war dragged on, the worse I got. Reluctantly, I got out of bed and opened the shutters. Dense fog shrouded the mountain, making for a drab morning. The weather matched my mood. The smell of impending rain used to make me sigh with contentment because it would mean lazy days when I could draw. Now it just made me angry because I would have to slog through the mud puddles that would fill my shoes. I can't stand the sound of mud squishing between my toes. I watched Ellie from the window and felt stupid for even thinking how much I hated muck. She had lost her beloved husband, and not once had I heard her complain. She asked God for the strength to endure. There's a special place in heaven for people like Elisavet.

I watched her sitting on the edge of the lookout, her feet dangling over the side. How long had she been out there? I decided that I needed some company before I became a cranky old woman. Ellie turned when she heard the door open and smiled at me.

"Did you sleep well?"

"I kept dreaming about killing the traitor."

"The traitor is already dead."

"If they buried him in the grove, I'm going to unbury him and haul his carcass across the valley and up this mountain."

Ellie must have found that amusing because I could see she was trying valiantly not to laugh. The corners of her mouth twitched.

"I'm serious, Elisavet!"

"Oh, I know you are because you used my full name, and you had your serious face on."

We smiled. I could never stay angry with anything when Ellie was around. I had missed her so much.

"I have this mental image of you hauling the traitor's fat body up Athena's Bluff, and it's amusing."

"I would do it, and have you wondered why, while everyone is starving and looking like skeletons, this gargantuan oaf was fat? Who stays fat in a famine?"

"I haven't spent any time thinking about why he was fat. I'm curious; what would you do once you got him up here?"

"Chop his head off, set fire to him, and throw him off the mountain."

"Would that ease your grief?"

I shook my head. "He doesn't deserve to be buried on Lambros sacred ground."

"A cemetery is not sacred ground."

"It is for me. Heroes are buried there. He deserves to be eaten by dogs."

"Doesn't do any good. My Angel is still dead."

I sat down next to her on the edge of the lookout. "God is cruel." I didn't mean to blurt that out, but it came out of my mouth, and there was nothing I could do about it.

"It would appear that way, but He's not. Man is cruel and debases himself." Ellie took my hand and held it. "I love you for being angry about Angelos's murder. He loved you a great deal. He wouldn't want you to harden your heart against the Lord."

"Too late. It's already as hard as a rock."

"You're scared and angry. It's all right to be scared. We all are. When you were younger, you used to get very angry when something bad happened to someone."

"I did?"

"Oh, yes. You threw things around, and you raged against everything. It wasn't because you were a tempestuous child; it was because you felt helpless. I understand why you are raging against God over Angel's murder." Ellie kissed me on the cheek. "It's why I love you so much. You care so deeply that you want to lash out at the unfairness."

"It's just not fair."

"Nothing in war is fair. We get up in the morning and hope we live for another day and possible liberation."

"I'm finding myself angry with everything, including my best pencil."

"You find yourself in a position you have no control over. It's not just you that is feeling this way."

"You don't lose your temper, and you seem so calm."

"I'm not calm. I'm a raging inferno inside, but there is nothing I can do about it. I have to lean on the Lord to get me through this."

"What if you have no faith in him?" I pointed heavenward. "Who do you lean on then?"

"Faith in Him has a way of coming back. You must have patience, and we know you have an abundance of that!" Ellie chuckled and playfully tapped me on the head with her fingers. "Now, why don't you go wash up? I'll find some rabbits for breakfast."

"Can we have a whole rabbit this time?"

Ellie laughed and picked up my crossbow, and it was then she noticed the name on the side. She smiled. "Arty would be so proud of that."

"I'm not quite sure if she would have liked her name on a crossbow, especially when I'm hunting, but I did it to honor her."

"She knows why you did that, Zo. I'm going to take Artemis to the hunt," she said, and playfully shadow shot arrows towards the brush. She smiled at me and headed for the bushes.

I stood at the outcrop and looked over the valley. I had so much rage, and I needed an outlet. I looked back at the cabin, and I knew what I had to do. Before I turned away, I looked up into the heavens and made a promise. "I will avenge your death, Angelos. A promise is a promise."

CHAPTER 26

Ellie took a great deal of time to return back from hunting for our breakfast. I had occupied my time by cleaning; it was the only way I could stop my mind from focusing on the traitor and hoping they had strung him up a tree. I cleaned the cabin from top to bottom and proceeded to scrub the floor outside. I was trying to get the rabbit's blood out of the timber, a useless exercise if ever there was one. I had contemplated the enormous task of emptying the water tank next to the cabin and was going to get inside it and give it a good clean. Cleaning occupied my mind and didn't leave time to ponder on things that would enrage me. The weather also had cleared up considerably, and I was getting worried about how long Ellie was taking to get back. I didn't have to worry for long because Ellie made a lot of noise as she came through the scrub.

"I found breakfast!"

I looked up, hoping she had found a rabbit, but instead, Ellie stood there looking quite pleased with herself. There was no rabbit in sight. If she had it in the sack, it was going to be a tiny animal.

"I wouldn't sound so happy if I returned with nothing to show for it."

"Patience, ZoZo, patience!"

I had returned to my scrubbing but stopped soon after when I found a clay pot placed right in front of me.

"You must have some faith!" Ellie said and lifted the lid.

I couldn't believe it. Ellie had found a pot of tarhana out in the woods! It was one of my favorite soups; my mother would dry fermented wheat with yogurt and let it dry out for days. It was quite a long process, but the soup that eventuated was scrumptious and filling. I knew where Ellie had found it. There was only one person who made these ornate pots; they were the creations of an old woman, Aikaterine Kaliopes, that lived about a mile down from Athena's Bluff. "You found yiayia Kaliopes! That woman is as old as the mountains."

"I was surprised she was still alive!" Ellie quipped, making me laugh.

"I worry about her, and every time I suggest she move into town, yiayia Kaliopes tells me that she was born in the woods, and this is where she will die."

"I tried to persuade her to come with us to the farm, but she told me that no one bothers her. I was near her property, and she came out with a rifle and almost shot my head off. Once she saw me, she invited me and gave me the pot!"

"Of course, she gave you the food because she loves you." I laughed and got up off the floorboards. I took the pot inside the cabin, and Ellie followed.

"Wow," Ellie exclaimed. "This is spotless!"

"I took out my anger on the dirt."

I found some bowls, and we took our breakfast to sit outside since the weather had improved. We ate in silence until my patience ran out. "You have to teach me to fight," I said and wiped my mouth with the back of my sleeve. Ellie gave me a disapproving look; I wasn't sure if it was my table manners or the 'teaching me' part that annoyed her.

"You have skills that are best used in less—"

"I told you I don't want to sit and watch."

"You need to have patience."

"Patience wasn't the problem with that soldier in the grove. If it weren't for you, he would have killed me."

"You can't run headlong into a soldier and expect him to fall over when you connect with your head."

That hadn't been my best moment, and there was nothing I could say, so I shrugged. Ellie wasn't mean. She was honest with me, and she was right. I had no fighting skills.

"I'm useless."

"You're not useless. You're an excellent huntress; I've seen you hunt. You have skills that none of the soldiers have."

"How to run fast?"

Ellie smiled. "No. It's the gift that the Lord gave us, Zoe. Your mother, my father, you, and me. We have it, and we must use it in this fight."

"What use is a good memory when I can't defend myself?"

"You can defend yourself, but when you are surprised,

you freeze. That's natural. Hardened soldiers freeze in battle. I've seen it, and they are older and well trained."

"Really?"

"Oh, yes." I expected Ellie to laugh, but she didn't. She was serious. She wasn't the type to say things just to hear herself talk.

"Can you train me?"

"You are not tall enough or quick enough to go into battle with soldiers..."

"Teach me."

"Zoe..."

"Teach me."

"I can show you how to fight, but what if you are asked to do something else other than fighting? Would you offer yourself up for the job I've wanted you to take on?"

"Does it involve the enemy?"

"It does."

"Show me how to fight first. At least I'll know how to do something besides running headlong into the enemy."

"You give me your word that you will take me up on the offer of what I had in mind?"

"I don't know what that is yet."

"Trust me, you will want to be involved in this."

I sighed. "What is it?" I put the bowl aside and gave my full attention to Ellie, who had her back braced against a boulder.

"I'm going to tell you something that very few people know. The Resistance is growing..."

"That's old news. I already figured that out."

"You haven't figured out anything. Can I explain this to you before you are so sure that you know everything?"

I playfully zipped my mouth and nodded for Ellie to continue. There are moments when I can shut up.

"I belong to two Resistance groups, and they both have different goals..."

"Liberation of Greece." I wasn't shutting up, and I just shrugged. "Sorry."

Ellie gazed at me for a moment before she continued. "One of the groups is small, for now, and we have been working in sabotaging the Germans and the Italians. Up to now, we have been like annoying insects, but our mission is going to change."

"You're going to be more like deadly insects?"

"You could say that. Our mission is to take out Busto."

Ellie stopped talking and waited. If I understood what she had just said, it would mean a significant escalation in our war against the Italians in Larissa. Busto wasn't just an Italian soldier—he was the vicious beast in command of the troops stationed in Larissa. "Busto is going to be assassinated? That is what you are saying, right?"

"Yes."

"How?"

"You."

My eyes must have looked like two large saucers because I was taken totally off guard. "Me? You want *me* to kill Busto?"

"No, we want *you* to use your gifts and watch what they do and when they do it."

"That's not that hard to figure out. Just stick someone outside and let them monitor the situation."

Ellie shook her head. "It's not that easy. The Italians know who lives near where Busto has his headquarters.

Michael's house is only a few doors down from there. No one is going to question you if they see you outside. You've been in the area many times."

"You don't want me to do anything other than sit and watch? That's not fighting, Ellie."

"I didn't say you would be fighting. The Resistance is not about close combat with the enemy. It's a delicate dance. They won't suspect you, and you look pretty harmless," Ellie said mischievously. "They won't know how dangerous you are, and that is to our advantage."

"How am I dangerous? All I have to do is sit outside and remember things."

"No." Ellie patted me on the knee and smiled. "You're dangerous because you can recall everything you see. Then we can plan our strategy around that."

"Oh."

"Your reconnaissance will lead to Busto's execution. Don't you think that's being part of the fight?"

"I'm not directly involved."

Ellie put her hand on my shoulder and gently squeezed. "The time will come for you to go into combat, but it's not on this mission. I told the leader of my cell that you are the perfect person for the job."

"What if I decline your offer?"

"I don't believe you will." Ellie shook her head. "It's a lot more complicated, but it's not the time to outline what we have in mind. For now, that is your mission. I can't promise that you will be given another role because I don't know. Are you interested?"

I hesitated because that wasn't what I wanted to do. I was going to try one more time to convince Ellie about training me and what I wanted to do in the Resistance. "Hear me out, please." I held Ellie's gaze. "I know what I want to do. I didn't know before, and you said it yourself, when I don't have a goal, I'm rudderless."

"Well, I didn't actually..."

"I need a mission that doesn't have me just watching patrols and reporting them to whoever. I need to get involved. I need to do something that will get them out of our country. I couldn't do it for Sterina, but I can do it for others."

"If you let me speak..."

"You're only going to tell me that I'm too young, and I have to watch the patrols, and I need—" Ellie put her hand over my mouth.

"If I take my hand away, will you stop talking long enough for me to tell you what else I have in mind for you?"

I nodded. Ellie held my gaze for a moment before she took her hand away. "Please, stop talking." She pulled me back down on the seat and held my hand. "You will be a formidable force once trained. You're already unstoppable when you set your mind on something, and I'm not sorry for any German or Italian soldier who crosses your path. I want to ask you a serious question. Think about what you are going to say."

"I already know the answer to the question."

"You haven't heard the question yet! Patience. I want to keep you safe, and if you are going to go further, you must think about what I'm about to say. Now, being in the Resistance is fraught with danger for obvious reasons, and the likelihood you may die is more than a possibility..."

"I know the dangers."

"No, you don't. Be quiet and listen. It's not just the possibility of getting killed, but also what happens if you are caught."

"What if I look at an Italian soldier the wrong way while walking down the road? I could end up dead. There are many ways to die in this war."

"Zoe..."

"Last week, I saw four men executed for trying to steal from the Italians. Let's not talk about how stupid those men were, but they weren't even in the Resistance."

"Here we go again... You must stop talking long enough..."

"Or I could end up starving to death or—" Once again, Ellie put her hand over my mouth."

"Theo was right; that's the only way to stop you talking. We should unleash you on the Italians, and you could talk them to death."

I did not find that funny, although it amused Ellie by the way she was chuckling. She took a sip from her cup and sighed. I was dismayed by the way the conversation was going.

"I find this whole conversation unfair. Why are you interrogating me?"

"You honestly think this is an interrogation?" Ellie asked, incredulously. She blew out a frustrated breath and shook her head. "Do you *know* what interrogation means?"

"Yes, I do. It's what you're doing to me."

"Oh, Lord." Ellie ran her hands through her curly hair and looked up into the darkened sky. "Zoe, I know you are angry, but you're not a dumb girl. You're intelligent and know what's at stake. When you get angry, you can't be reasoned with. This isn't an interrogation."

"Did you ask Stelios what he would do if he ever got caught?"

"No, but—"

"What about Stavros? Do you ask all the other members of your Resistance cell about their motives for joining?

"Let me explain..."

"Oh, I know why you are asking me. Mama told you to dissuade me from joining the Resistance."

"Is that right? Are we talking about the same woman who let you go out in the fields to hunt, knowing the dangers?

"Yes, but—"

"The woman that could have said no but instead chose to put you in danger because she knew it was for the right reason? The woman—"

"I understand. You don't need to pound me on the head."

"No, you don't understand anything. Could your mother have prevented you from going out with Stavros?"

"No... I mean... yes."

"By your reasoning, you think your mother asked me to dissuade you from joining the Resistance? How weak do you think your mother is?"

"She's not weak."

"Exactly. Your mother knows you better than you know yourself. She knows that you have wanted to join the Resistance since the war began. She also knows that if you are not brought into the cell, you will run off into the mountains to join a group there."

"No, I would never do that," I replied indignantly. "Tell me why you are questioning me this way." I got up and started to pace. My patience had evaporated and been replaced by resentment and a rising fear that I wasn't ever going to have a chance to prove my worth.

"You are a hothead, Zoe. Sit back down here."

"No."

Ellie sighed. "Sit. Down."

I wanted to disobey her, but if I did that, Ellie would use it as a strike against me, and I would be relegated to watching patrols for the rest of the war. Reluctantly, I sat back down and folded my arms in defiance.

Ellie gazed at me, and then I realized what she was doing. "Mama didn't tell you that I would run off into the mountains if she told me not to get involved, did she?"

"No, she didn't. You would never abandon your mother even if you passionately wanted to join the Resistance. Your mother did talk to me, and she asked me to make sure that you knew what was at stake and to share with you the mission about Busto."

"I was right; she did talk to you."

"Of course she talked to me, Zoe. I approached her first about this mission and wanted to know if I could ask you. I wouldn't ask Stelios's mother because he's a grown man and doesn't need her permission. I asked my father to get Stav involved. You're not the exception, even though you think you are."

"What did she say?"

"She was worried that you didn't know the ramifications. What if everyone you love is killed? What will you do?"

"Fight..." I replied and was going to continue until I remembered a story my mother used to tell me that crystallized what my answer would be. "Mama told me a story about our Spartan ancestors and the bravery they had. She said that before the Spartan soldiers went into battle, their mother would hand the shield to her son. She would urge him to come back with his shield or on his shield. If he came back with his shield, he was a hero because he fought bravely. If he came back on it, he died heroically. No Spartan ever came home without his shield because it would mean he had thrown it away in battle and run off like a coward."

"Yes, I have heard that story."

"There's my answer to your question. Yes, I could die. Yes, my mother could die, but so could you or Stavros. I could be captured and die a horrible death, but I choose to join the Resistance because I am a Greek, and I choose to fight or die trying. It's the Spartan way; *with* it or *on* it." No sooner had I replied that I realized that was what Ellie was trying to get through to me.

"I believe you would continue to fight. I believe it down to the marrow of my bones. I wanted you to realize what was at stake."

"No one can't protect me, Ellie. I *know* what's at stake. I know what the Italians and the Germans have done to women and young girls. I have ears and have heard the stories. I may be young, but I'm not stupid."

"You're not stupid; far from it..."

"I will never reveal who the rest of the Resistance is. I would never betray them."

"You can't..."

"What? I will never betray my brothers and sisters. Never."

"Remember the last night that Jesus was with his apostles at the Last Supper?"

I smiled. "Not really; I wasn't there."

Ellie flicked the back of my head with her fingers. "Do you remember reading how Jesus said to Peter that he would deny Him three times?"

"What does that have to do with what we are talking about?"

"I'll tell you shortly. Peter was adamant that he would never deny Jesus."

"Boy, was he wrong."

"Yes, but he was certain he would never do that to Jesus. Yet when the time came, Jesus had been right about Peter. Was Peter a traitor like Judas when he denied knowing his beloved friend three times?"

"No."

"Wouldn't that be a betrayal? All he got was a little interrogation from the mob, and he fell apart. It wasn't even an interrogation by the Romans."

"Peter is my favorite apostle, and he got scared. That doesn't make him a coward."

Ellie's lips twitched. "I know, and that's why I used Peter's moment of weakness to show you that being scared is not a sign you are..."

"If I'm captured, I won't deny Jesus three times," I joked and watched Ellie's eyebrows furrow in annoyance. "I'm aware of what will happen to me if I'm captured, and I know the dangers."

"You are never sure about anything once you've been captured, Zoe. No one knows how they will react."

I nodded and fully understood the comparison. I tried not to think of the Germans capturing me or anyone else who I loved.

"Do I have to pass any other test to get into your Resistance cell?"

"No. You were in the cell the moment you were born."

"Are you one of the Fates?"

Ellie chuckled and shook her head. "No, what I meant is that your passion and ferocity for your country is what we are looking for."

"Oh, well then, you're right. I've been ready since I was born! Does that mean my mission has changed, and I'm not a watcher?"

"No, it hasn't changed, but I will give you a chance to learn how to fight against a larger opponent."

"Yes. Now, tell me about the other Resistance group and why those two are not working together?"

"Take the bowls inside, and I will tell you."

CHAPTER 27

I came back from leaving the bowls in the kitchen and found that Ellie had not moved away from the ledge. I sat down and motioned for her to continue.

"I suggest you sit further back."

"Can you stop playing games and tell me?"

"I have a reason for saying that other than watching your exasperation with me. I'm going to tell you something that may make you accidentally throw yourself off the mountain." Ellie put her hand on my shoulder and laughed. "I want you to sit back away from the edge."

"Really? What would make me accidentally kill myself?"

Ellie didn't say a word. She just pointed for me to move away from the edge, and I did as she requested because I was eager to hear what she had to say. It was fun to see her this playful.

"All right. Now tell me."

"I belong to a Resistance group started by Lela Karagianni."

"I don't know her. She's not from Farsala."

"Lela is from Athens, and before you say all Athenians are lunatics, like your boyfriend Apostolos, hear me out."

"He's not my boyfriend. He shouldn't pay you to talk about him to me. Go ahead."

"Lela has set up a Resistance group that is effective. I met some of the members, and they recruited me after Angelos died."

"Are they the group that I met in the cave?"

"It would have been better if you hadn't seen them, but yes, that was my cell."

"Who is this Karagianni woman?"

Ellie smiled. "You didn't ask me what the group is called."

"I already know what it's called. It's the Karagianni Resistance group. It's not so exciting that I would have accidentally fallen off the mountain!"

Ellie laughed and put her hands over her head. "You make me laugh so much my head hurts. The group is called the Bouboulinas."

"As in Laskarina Bouboulina?"

"Yes, your heroine Laskarina."

"Are you serious?" If this was true, I wanted to join the Bouboulinas! That was the last thing I had expected. "You're not joking with me, are you?"

"No, I'm not joking. This Resistance group is called the Bouboulinas."

"Yes."

"Don't you want to find out what their mission is before you agree?"

I shook my head and grinned. "I am going to be a Bouboulina. That's all I need to know."

"Let me understand your reasoning. If I had told you that the Bouboulinas wanted you to be a lookout and not participate, like I did with the previous group, you would say yes without even hesitating?"

"Yes." I nodded furiously. That only made Ellie laugh, and for a moment, I thought she was going to fall off the mountain herself. "It's not that funny!"

"Yes, it is! I should have started telling you about the Bouboulinas!"

"You did, and it was a missed opportunity. I want to join the Bouboulinas. I don't care what it is."

"I thought you would enjoy that. When they told me what it was called, I thought of you."

"Well, it's easy to see why you would think of me."

Ellie chuckled and gazed at me fondly. "And why is that?"

"I've been telling everyone who wants to listen, and those that don't, that my hero is Laskarina since I was old enough to talk."

"Yes, you and Yiayia Maria, bless her."

"Tell me more. What do the Bouboulinas do?" I smiled at saying the name, causing Ellie to laugh even more. "I can't help it; the name is beautiful."

"I love you so much, Zoe. You are so easy to please. We help Allied soldiers and Jews to escape, and we do other things best left unsaid."

"Is that why you are here?"

"Initially, no. I came home because my soul needed to heal."

"How did you get involved with this Resistance group and the other one?"

"It's best not to know everything. That's for your safety and everyone else's. I trust you, but if you are captured... let's not talk about that."

"That explains Mama's actions. She's in the group as well, isn't she?"

"Yes. I recruited Aunty Helena and the rest of the family."

"You didn't recruit me." I was a little hurt about that. I tried not to show my disappointment, but I'm not very good at hiding my feelings.

"Is that what you think? Did you forget what I asked you to do and you agreed? Wasn't that recruiting you into the Resistance?"

"You asked Mama to join the Bouboulinas and not the other group, right?"

"It's not that clear cut. Everyone has a different role to play, and yours will be unlike what your mama will be doing."

"So, you want me to join both resistance groups then?" I stood up and began to pace."

Ellie was fighting hard not to start laughing at my enthusiastic response to her invitation. I didn't know what I was going to be doing for the Bouboulinas, but I didn't care. Any group that took its name from the greatest hero of the War of Liberation had to be involved in ridding our country of the enemy. I was trying to be calm about it, but I was getting more excited the longer I thought about it.

I broke out into a dance. It was fortunate that we were high up a mountain and relatively safe from the Italians with all the yelling I was doing. It was also lucky that I was not a heavy-set girl, because I could have broken the ledge with all the jumping I was doing.

"All right, settle down!" Ellie laughed at my antics. "Come back here and sit down."

"Not too close to the edge, or I might dance myself off the cliff!"

"Well, we wouldn't want that."

I sat back down and plastered a broad smile on my face. "I'm excited."

"You have a hard time showing your feelings, Zo," Ellie replied, making us laugh.

I leaned over and gave her a kiss on the cheek. "I won't disappoint you."

"I know. You will give it everything you have."

"I'm in the Bouboulinas!" I said in a sing-song voice and couldn't stop the laugh that bubbled forth. I put my hand over my mouth and giggled. We sat there in silence for a few minutes before I sobered up and turned to Ellie with the question I had wanted to ask since I woke up.

"Are we are going back to the farm?"

Ellie nodded. "Soon."

"How did you know who the traitor was? Was it the Resistance that found out?"

"It was something Aunty Stella said that made me question our traitorous uncle."

"Yes, but how did she know it was that piece of filth that did it?"

"I don't know, but she was right."

"Are you going to stay here for now?"

"Yes. We have work to do down here. There are Allied soldiers and Jews who need a way out of Thessaly."

"The Italians had the Jews in the camp near the river. Stavros and I went hunting, and we found some who had escaped. I couldn't save one of the women..."

"You couldn't save them, Zoe. They were going to die. There was nothing you could have done. Stavros told me what you did, and it was heroic." Ellie put her hand on my knee and tried to reassure me.

"I let Sterina down, and that was due to my inexperience and stupidity."

"You are young and inexperienced. You have never been in battle, and here you were confronted by a situation where you had to defend someone who was scared out of her mind."

"I need to be trained."

"Didn't I say that I will train you? With Sterina, you had no chance. We attempted to rescue them, but scared people who are looking for any chance to escape don't follow directions."

"Was your group behind their release?"

"Our group was, and we failed. You didn't."

"What about the little girl in the cave?"

"That was one of the children we rescued, but she ran off. Again, we failed." Ellie turned away from the edge of the lookout and sat cross-legged in front of me. "We have heard and seen the evilness of these beasts."

"Why isn't someone stopping them?"

"The world turns a blind eye to these atrocities. The

Germans can do whatever they want, and no one will question them."

"What about the Resistance?"

"We *are* the Resistance. We can save people, but we can't save everyone. Once the Germans take over…"

"Why will the Germans take over? The Italians are their allies."

"In war, everything changes, and the Germans want complete control."

"What will happen when they do?"

"The mass murder of Jews in Greece will begin. That's what will happen. That's what has happened in other countries under German occupation. We are getting stories of horrific atrocities—brutal crimes that are so cruel you would think they could not be human. We have demons walking amongst us."

"Uncle Ignatius rescued a woman and her daughter and brought them to the house…"

"Yes," Ellie nodded. "I know about that. The Bouboulinas were responsible for that, and we continue to save more people. We have a network of people to help the Jews escape."

"Laskarina would have been so proud of this group. The daughter's name was Esther, and she was my age. She told me about the Night of Crystal…"

"Kristallnacht," Ellie quietly said. "I know all about it. Two of Angel's best friends were murdered—one on the first night and the other on the second night."

"Oh, poor boys. Did the world know about this evil man?"

"They did."

"Why didn't they do something? Maybe they could have stopped the murders!" I asked in bewilderment.

Ellie nodded. "You have to remember that the world will act once they are threatened. They won't help us unless Hitler goes after them. That day will come, Zo."

"Not fast enough to save people."

"No, it never is fast enough. Our Allies are winning battles, and one day they will liberate Europe."

"It doesn't look like they are winning anything if they can't save people from being murdered."

"You can't save everyone. We must save as many people as we can and thwart the enemy."

"How do we do that?"

"We stop their murderous plans. We get the Jews to safety, and we disrupt their plans. We will do whatever needs to be done to stop them."

"I want to avenge Angel's murder and kill them for what they are doing to all Greeks."

"You are going to do that, Zo. You are our secret weapon." Ellie got up from the ledge, and she offered me her hand, and we both walked towards the cabin. Ellie sat down on the bench outside while I packed up my satchel.

"You didn't ask me what the name of the other group is," Ellie said while I was inside. I leaned outside to see her staring out towards the valley.

"Is there a reason you are concerned that I didn't ask? What is the group called?"

"The KKE."

I took a deep breath. It hit me like a bomb had gone off beside me. I dropped my satchel and stared at Ellie for a long moment. "Communists." I turned from Ellie and spat on the ground. "They murdered Uncle Vassili. How could you work with them?"

"I will work with the devil if it means we get people to safety and take back our country. This is more important than—"

"It's more important than Uncle Vassili?"

"Yes." Ellie put her hand on my shoulder. "We must work with whoever we can to get the job done. We must hold our nose and get the job."

"Would you work with the Nazis?" I regretted saying it the moment it left my mouth. I was upset at myself that I had let my anger override my love for my cousin. "I'm sorry, that was…"

"It's alright. I was anticipating your anger, and I despise the communists, but…"

"We will work with the devil himself to defeat the enemy."

"Are you going to change your mind about helping us?"

"No, I gave you my word that I will join you. I hate Busto more than I hate the communists. They're not my enemy, for now."

Ellie put her hand on my shoulder as we left the cabin and took the track through the scrub. We made our way down the mountain and reached the main road. Ellie arranged the entrance to appear as if there was no track behind it, and we set off down the road towards the farm.

CHAPTER 28

MAY 02, 1942

LARISSA

I sat outside on the top step of Michael's home and occupied myself by hemming pants and sewing buttons on shirts. I occasionally looked up towards the house on the corner. I would then resume my sewing. Soldiers would pass and give me a cursory glance and continue on their way towards the commander's house. When the earthquake struck, the row of houses leading to the commandeered quarters had been badly damaged, and they were nothing more than shells. I had an unobstructed view of the house of Busto and his soldiers.

Stavros and Giorgos, the man-mountain, had joined me at the house. They were there to repair non-existent damage from the earthquake. Giorgos was big and hairy, a true mountain boy, and his shirts were the size of bedsheets.

Stavros wasn't short by any measure, but Giorgos made him look like a little boy. If any Italian soldier tried to get inside, they would be met by the human Mount Olympus. No one ever tried to do that, and I was a little disappointed, not because I wanted Italians in my home but because I missed out on the sight of Giorgos in full flight.

The surveillance had been going on for a few weeks, and in that time, Busto would leave and return at the same time. At first, it amused me, and then it intrigued me as to where he was going. I could set my watch by him.

One day we created a diversion to get an Allied soldier away from the area. He had been hidden in one of the earthquake-damaged houses, and the only escape route was to get past Busto's headquarters and the soldiers guarding the property. We had tried getting him out at night but there were extra patrols in the area and additional checkpoints had been set for some reason. I was sure the Italians would find the poor man but they were oblivious of his whereabouts. We had to come up with a better plan. The longer he was hidden, the more chance he would be discovered.

Our job was simple enough; we were to be the diversion, and I'm quite good at making a fool of myself. I started to sing loudly, off-key, and dancing on the seat of my bicycle while I rode towards Michael's house. In my exuberance, I 'lost' control of my bike and rode straight into Giorgos. I didn't think the Italians would believe that something that silly would happen, but I was wrong. The soldiers on the other side of the street started laughing and their attention was diverted from what they were supposed to be doing. I didn't have to wonder how they lost in Albania; they were just plain stupid.

I never knew what it was like to slam into solid rock, but I felt it that day. I tried not to take any notice of a couple of old 'women' clad in black, their heads covered by scarves that were shuffling our way. The closer they got, the more nervous I became. Just as the old ladies were going to pass behind us, I started waving my arms and jumping up and down because something had bitten me. That part was real, and I wasn't acting although that did get another round of uproarious laughter from the Italians, and it even had Stavros laughing so much; he had to steady himself against a tree. I knew it was genuine because every time he would look at me, he would start up again. It's been a while since my cousin laughed so much and that made me feel good as well.

We were relieved that our ruse worked and it was right on time because if we had started our diversion just a little later, it would have been disastrous for everyone. After I had stopped acting the fool, I spotted something further up the street. Coming up the side road was a group of German soldiers in formation.

"Nazis," Stavros whispered.

"How can you tell?" They looked like regular soldiers to me. I was relieved our old ladies had disappeared around the corner and were not in any danger.

Stavros leaned down and whispered in my ear. "Look at their helmets. They have the SS on them. They're Nazi soldiers."

"What does the SS stand for?"

"Schutzstaffel," Giorgos said. "They are elite soldiers. I've seen them in Thessaloniki."

"What are they doing here?"

No sooner had I asked that when I saw a black car come up behind the soldiers and then go around them to stop in front of the house. A Nazi officer and Busto came out of the vehicle. "That's interesting."

"No, it's not interesting; it means trouble," Giorgos said. "That's SS Major Bonhoffen."

"Zoe Lambros!"

I heard my name and turned away from the Nazis to see Kiria Despina coming up the street. The poor woman had been given the job of being Busto's housekeeper. I was about to greet her when she grabbed me by the arm and forced me to go along with her. "You're coming with me."

"I can't. I have to stay…"

"You are coming with me." That was all she said and dragged me by the arm. I turned to look at Stavros and shrugged. We passed the soldiers in front of Busto's house, and they waved us through. Italians are such idiots.

I had been told I was going into the house at some point, but I didn't know when this was going to take place. I just found out how I was going to pass through without the Italians suspecting. Not only that, but I was in the house when the notorious Bonhoffen was present.

Kiria Despina gave me some rags and told me to go clean the house. The fools had no idea that by allowing me access to the house, I could quickly draw it and give the drawing to my comrades. I was about to head up the steps when I caught sight of Bonhoffen through an open door. His hand went to his gun, and I thought he had found out who I was and was going to shoot me, but he pointed the gun at someone in the room and fired. The entrance hall was flooded with soldiers but there was nothing for them to do. Bonhoffen had shot one of his soldiers. He didn't even get out of his chair.

I quickly walked up the steps to the sound of Bonhoffen laughing, and it made me shudder.

CHAPTER 29

MAY 05, 1942

FARSALA

Ugh.

I had spent more time spitting out dirt than training to fight. I was terrible at this, but I wasn't ready to give up. I was going to continue until I managed to find myself halfway competent.

My "assailant" offered me his hand, and I took it. Uncle Petros effortlessly hauled me up and made me feel like the child I was.

"You were better this time, ZoZo, just next time kick and then run," Uncle Petros admonished, and I nodded for the umpteenth time.

My whole body ached from the various ways I found to end up on the ground. I did want to learn how to fight, didn't I? I hobbled over to a chair and sat down. I had twisted my ankle in the last "fight," and now I was feeling it every time I walked. Feeling like a failure was becoming something I was getting used to.

"Can I sit, or would you rather berate yourself some more?"

I looked up to find Ellie staring down at me. I motioned for her to pull up an overturned crate and sit beside me.

"You can say it now."

"That last kick was impressive, but his crotch is a little higher than his knees."

"You're so funny."

"I know, but no one else thinks so except you." Ellie ruffled my hair, which dislodged pieces of bark and dirt. "You need a bath, ZoZo."

"Ha, ha."

"Can we call it a day on your hand-to-hand combat?"

"I'm useless at being a Resistance member. Maybe you should rethink your idea of me joining the Bouboulinas."

"I told you that you are too small for the hand-to-hand combat stuff. Men are bigger than you, and they will always overpower you. I'll tell you a secret. You wouldn't have taken my father down easily. Stav can't take him down, and my brother is a big boy, as you can see."

"I think you forgot to mention that when you paired us up," I said sarcastically. It was true my uncle was a tall and broad-shouldered man, and when I was directed to train with him, I thought my life would end if he used all his strength against me. I knew he wouldn't do that but my anxiety over facing a larger opponent was not lessened by the fact that my uncle wasn't trying to hurt me.

"You won't come up against just short men; more than likely, they will be bigger and stronger than you."

"Everyone keeps saying that." I blew out an exasperated breath.

"Don't get angry because the Lord made you small. He gave you other gifts..."

"I know, I know, but those gifts are not useful in a fight."

"Well, that's the most stupid thing I've ever heard come out of your mouth." Ellie put her arm around me and knocked on my head with her fingers. "Hello, can you let Zoe come out to play, please?"

"Don't mock me; it's not nice."

"Look at me." Ellie tapped me on the nose. I turned my head and found her smiling at me. "I'm not mocking you. You are too small for combat."

"How tall was Joan of Arc?" I asked, knowing the answer already.

Ellie's smile widened. "I thought you were going to ask me how tall Laskarina was. Joan was shorter than you."

"She led an army and fought with a sword. She wasn't built for battle, and she was shorter than me."

"That's true, she was. I'm sure if you look back into history, you will find a lot of women who were shorter than you and were warriors. They trained for many years to get proficient in combat. You don't have that much time. The point here is that your role in the Resistance is not to be involved in hand-to-hand combat. You have a different role." I understood what Ellie was trying to say, but I was disappointed in myself.

"You are proficient with the crossbow, with a knife, and I've seen you shoot. What you can't do is give the man the leverage he needs to defeat you. Use your height to your advantage."

"That would be great if I loaded my crossbow quickly. I almost killed myself against the soldier in the forest because I didn't load fast enough."

Ellie gently tapped me on the side of my head. "Use your head. If you can't use your crossbow, go for your gun. If you can't use the gun, go for the knife. If your knife is not available, use whatever is around you. Improvise. Use the man's height against him."

"I could stomp on his foot and run."

"I'm going to stop you right there. Since when did you become such a defeatist? You've been phenomenal with the surveillance on Busto, and the information on Bonhoffen was invaluable. Your mission has ended, and now we start you on another mission."

"When is Busto going to die?"

"I don't know, and that's not my concern." Ellie shook her head. "I need your hunting skills. More to the point, I need your pinpoint accuracy."

"Have you forgotten that I missed when I shot that soldier?"

"That was the first time you were in a fight with the enemy. All soldiers freeze. I told you that. If you ask any of the men here, they will tell you that is what happens. It's nothing to be ashamed of." Ellie put her hand on my shoulder. "Everyone freezes."

"What do I do?"

"You find their crotch, and you kick it," Ellie responded, making me laugh. "Trust me, that's their weakness. Once you kick their manhood, they will go down faster than a speeding bullet. You're holding back from kicking or gouging eyes. You're not a timid girl, and yet you hesitate."

"I'm not fighting the enemy right now. I don't want to hurt them."

"The boys will live if you kick them. Now, are you ready for me to show you what I want you to do? Pick up your crossbow, and let's go." Ellie pulled me up by the hand and led me away.

I was going to ask where we were going, but for once, I chose to shut my mouth and waited to be told. We ended up on the road leading to the farm. There was a slight bend as the road curved, which was obscured by trees on either side.

"This road is similar to the place we will be attacking a convoy of trucks."

"Where are they coming from?"

"Athens." Ellie's smile widened, and she took several steps back from me—a move I found very odd.

"Are you going to tell me to not fall off a mountain again?" I said and laughed when Ellie nodded vigorously.

"It's in Lamia."

I was stunned into silence and, for a moment, I thought I might have hit my head on the ground too many times, and my ears were not working. "What did you say?"

"You heard me the first time. I said we are going to Lamia."

I was feeling lightheaded and promptly sat down in the tall grass. "The trucks would be coming through the pass at Thermopylae."

"That is the usual route."

I looked up into Ellie's sparkling green eyes that were gazing down at me. "You're sending me into battle at Thermopylae," I said in amazement.

"No, it's not at Thermopylae..."

"It's just outside the pass of Thermopylae."

"Yes."

"Oh, I'm going to be sick." I quickly lay down and put my hands over my eyes. Ellie joined me on the ground and chuckled. I turned my head to find she was lying on her side with the biggest grin on her face. "What do you want me to do? Tie everyone's shoelaces? Make food? Anything. I'll do anything to go to Thermopylae." I put up my hand to forestall Ellie's imminent interruption. "One meter out of the pass of Thermopylae, I don't care. I'm going into battle at Thermopylae." I put my hand over my forehead and started to giggle. "I wish Arty was here to see this."

"Oh, no, not Thermopylae again! You won't get her to shut up for the rest of her life!" Ellie mimicked her sister, causing both of us to laugh because Ellie sounded exactly like Arty, so much so that it made me happy and sad at the same time. "I wish she were here too so she can see your goofy grin." Ellie chuckled and drummed her fingers on my head. "I love how excited you get. Do you want to go on this mission?"

"I do." I said and nodded so vigorously, I thought my head would be disengaged from my neck and roll away in the grass..

"You won't think it's unimportant that you may be just sitting around…"

"I can be a lookout! I don't care. Send me in! Please can I go?"

"Of course you can go, that's why I told you."

I rolled onto my side, and we faced each other in the tall grass. "Are you serious, I'm going to Thermopylae?"

"I think I've mentioned this, haven't I? We're going to Lamia, but it's coming from Thermopylae."

My face hurt from smiling so much. "I meant it when I said..."

"Zoe, you're not going to cook or tie anyone's shoelaces. I have a special mission for you."

"Oh." I had a mission. At Thermopylae. I was ecstatic but also apprehensive. "How many of the group know?"

"Not everyone. I told you because I trust you. As I said, I have a special role for you to play. We don't have a lot of time to train for this. We got word this morning that the tracks out of Athens were damaged."

"Blown up?"

"Unfortunately not, but the line was damaged. It will slow down the Germans but not for long. We need to be ready to ambush the trucks that are coming through in three days."

"How do we know it's going to take three days? Won't they repair the damage quicker than that?"

"Don't worry about that. We have to worry about the mission."

"How do we know they are coming through Lamia?"

"How we know is not important right now. We don't have a lot of time because our window for attacking the convoy is small. Give me your crossbow."

I willingly gave her my weapon, and we got up from the ground. Ellie motioned to someone that was sitting in a truck to move forward. She dropped down near the tall grass. "You need to wait for the truck to round the bend."

"What am I going to be doing?"

"Killing the driver and his passenger in the first truck."

I took a deep breath and thought about how I was going to achieve that. "I can't blow out the tires because the arrows won't pierce through the rubber."

"I know." Ellie nodded, and we waited for the truck to get to the point where Ellie indicated for the vehicle to stop. "When the truck rounds the bend, there will be a lot of debris on the road. The truck will have to stop. At this point, you take over." She rose from the tall grass and rested on one knee. She aimed and pretended to shoot into the truck."

"You want me to kill the driver and his passenger with my arrows. Why not shoot them?"

"That will alert the other trucks that are behind them."

"So, my job is to hide, rise, and shoot."

"Yes, and it has to be within seconds of them stopping. I need your accuracy. The road is narrow, and I want you to stop them cold."

"What about the other trucks?"

"Don't worry about the other trucks. We need the first one to stop quietly and not to alert the others. Can you do that?"

"I can do that." I was confident that I was up to the task. I looked up at Ellie, who was looking at me rather oddly. "What?"

"You didn't ask why we are doing this."

"To kill Germans."

"No, that's not the mission, although Germans will die."

Ellie took my hand and led us back to the tall grasses, where we sat down. "Do you remember what I said about the Bouboulinas and their role in the Resistance?"

"To save Jews and Allied soldiers."

"Yes. This convoy will be carrying Jewish children away from Athens to Thessaloniki. The pass-through Thermopylae is the quickest route." Ellie put her arm around my shoulders.

"How do I save the children?"

"The first truck will have Jewish children in the back..."

"Does it matter what faith the children are? They are Greek and that's all that matters."

Ellie's face creased in the broadest smile. "I simply adore you, Zoe Lambros!" Ellie put her arms around me and gave me a kiss on the cheek. "I'm happy you are on our side because the Germans won't know what hit them."

"That's a little over the top but all right." I giggled. "Are you sure that the children will be in the first truck? How do we know?"

"That's the information we got. Your job is to kill the driver and the soldier beside him, then you will lead the children to safety. For now, that's all you need to know."

I'm usually not at a loss for words, but at that moment, I was struck mute by the sheer magnitude of the mission. I was going to be responsible for leading children to safety. This plan was audacious, and it terrified me, but it also made things that much clearer.

"Take a breath," Ellie said softly. "You can do this. The Lord has prepared you for this role, Zoe. There was a reason you learned to hunt and shoot. The Lord was guiding you to this moment. You and the angels will get this done."

"Is this a bad time to tell you that I don't trust God?"

Ellie's chuckle made me smile despite my rising anxiety. "It's all right, He trusts you. That's all that matters."

"That's my mission in this war—to save Jews, isn't it?"

"Your mission is not just to save Jews."

"Yes, it is, because I must avenge the deaths of Angel and Arty."

"You alone cannot avenge their deaths, but by saving Jews and our soldiers, their deaths will not be in vain. How do you feel about that?"

"I've found my purpose and I know what I have to do now."

"I knew you would. It's time for the new Spartans to go into battle at Thermopylae."

"Thermopylae," I said in awe of the legendary place seeped in Greek history. For the first time since the war started, I didn't feel helpless. I wasn't useless. I had found my purpose in the Resistance.

CHAPTER 30

MAY 08, 1942

FARSALA

Sleep was an elusive beast. Leading up to our time to leave for Domokos and then Lamia, Morpheus was not doing his mythical job of sending me into dreamland. The closer the day approached, the worse I felt. I had so much nervous energy that I even practiced in the dark.

I could load my crossbow with my eyes closed.

I dry fired my gun and practiced loading it and unloading it.

I threw my knife at a target until my shoulder ached.

Can you prepare too much?

There was no use in going to bed since, in a few hours, we would be heading out. We were setting off on foot so as not to arouse any suspicion. We were going to meet up with the second group in Domokos. I hoped we had a wagon because it was going to be a long walk to Lamia if we didn't.

I heard a noise behind me and turned to find my mother standing in the doorway. She didn't say anything but closed the door behind her and took a seat beside me.

"On the night before your Papa was to take the Australians over the gorge, we sat here and talked."

"Was Papa scared?"

"No, your Papa was confident he could get the men to safety, and of course, I was scared he would never make it back."

"Papa was a brave man. Braver than I am."

"Nonsense," Mama replied and pulled me towards her. I ended up lying across the bench with my head on her lap. "None of my children are cowards. I am proud of you and your brothers."

"What if I am a coward, and the only way we find out is if..."

"You will never be a coward, little one. I knew this to be a fact before you were born. You fought to stay alive inside me, and you fought when you were born."

"That's why you named me Zoe!"

"You had so much life in you that every other name didn't fit you. You're lucky we didn't listen to Theo because he wanted us to name you Calypso."

"Ugh. Why?"

My mother chuckled. "His dog was named Calypso."

The story made me laugh because it was something Theo would have done. He was ten years old when I was born.

"I was having so many problems while I carried you, I

thought for sure we would lose you. You didn't give up and kept on fighting. Your papa called you 'little Laskarina.' On the day you were born, your deliriously happy father climbed onto the roof of the house and started yelling how much he loved his little Laskarina!"

"I'm surprised you didn't name me Laskarina."

"Giving you the name of one of the greatest Resistance fighters in all of Greece would have been a huge burden to carry."

We sat in silence as I contemplated telling my mother what terrified me the most. I glanced at her, and I realized that she knew. My mother always knew what I was feeling.

"How do you know I won't fail?"

"Have you prayed to God to give you strength?

Why did my mother ask me a question whose answer she already knew? I made no secret of my disdain for God. I looked at her and shook my head. "It's out of his hands."

"Be anxious for nothing, but in everything by prayer and supplication, with thanksgiving, let your requests be made known to God." My mother recited the bible, something that wasn't hard to predict.

"God doesn't listen to my prayers."

"Trust in the Lord with all your heart and lean not on your own understanding; in all your ways submit to him, and he will make your paths straight."

"Did you memorize the entire Bible?" I gently teased, making my mother quietly chuckle.

"The Bible gives me hope, my darling. I know you are scared, and I would be worried if you were overconfident." Mama took my hand and held it tightly. "Being scared is normal."

"What if I freeze as I did in the forest?"

"You won't. You didn't freeze when the Italian soldier was running after you," Mama reminded me. "You outran him. You used your head and didn't make the mistakes you made in the forest."

"I don't want to let everyone down."

"You won't. I'm proud of you, my baby girl. Papa is also proud of you."

"Let's hope I don't get to hear him say that in a few days," I joked, and regretted it the moment I saw the tears glistening in my mama's eyes. I can be so stupid sometimes.

"I will pray for God to keep you safe and for you to come back to me."

She hugged me fiercely, and I needed to feel her love. She kissed me on the cheek and sniffed back the tears.

"I've put some clean underwear in your pack."

That was the last thing I was expecting my mother to say, and I burst out laughing. I glanced at my mama, who was also smiling. If anyone had seen us, they would have thought us mad. They were tears of happiness, sadness, and sheer terror.

It was close to the time that I had to leave, and as I got up from my seat, my mother pulled me down and hugged me tightly.

"You are a Greek soldier going to fight at Thermopylae, my daughter, just like our ancestors. God is on our side." I wonder if the Spartans felt so much fear and if Mama remembered what happened to them at Thermopylae.

CHAPTER 31

LAMIA, NEAR THERMOPYLAE

We silently assembled—Stavros, Giorgos and me. We were almost like spirits in the night. We were ready for battle. The second group would go soon after us and meet at Domokos before we all traveled to Lamia. We walked away from the farm in the darkness, and I didn't want to look back, but when we reached the top of the crossroads, I glanced back and saw Mama still standing at the gate. What was she thinking of when she saw her only daughter going to war? I was heading to a battle that I may not survive. I took one long last look at my mother before I turned and walked away.

It was time to prove myself. Our journey was slow until we reached Domokos, and we quickly made our way to a cave to await the second and third groups. The waiting was excruciating.

Once we were all together, we had to wait for our transport. When it arrived, we were once again on the move, and this time the journey took less time. I stood at the mouth of the cave that overlooked the valley.

Here I was in the old battleground that my ancestors fought in—the mountains of Thermopylae. If I hadn't been so scared and terrified of letting everyone down, I would have loved the idea of being where King Leonidas stared down the Persians. Three hundred men against the might of the Persian army. I wondered what those men thought about when they looked out into the same valley.

I had been to Thermopylae with my brothers after I had badgered them about visiting the site of King Leonidas' heroic deeds. They usually ignored my pleas, but I wore them down, and they took me. I stood at the pass that King Leonidas defended and eventually lost, and I was the happiest ten-year-old in all of Greece.

I was thinking of useless things like a centuries-old dead king who lost at Thermopylae and making myself sick with worry. I took Artemis out of my bag and cleaned her. I felt a sickening churning sensation and wanted to throw up but held it back because the others were fast asleep, and the last thing they needed was to worry about a child being sick. We needed to rest before everyone arrived in the early hours of the morning.

Spiro was keeping guard. He smiled and went back to staring into the darkness, his rifle at the ready.

All the talk about bravery and wanting to be in the Resistance came down to this. It was time for me to show what I was made of. I must be like Laskarina Bouboulina, and I needed the bravery of my Spartan ancestors. '*With* it or *on* it' was their saying. I held my crossbow in my hands and made the decision that I was going back home '*with* it' rather than '*on* it.' Now that my mind was where it should be, I needed to sleep. Just as I was about to move back, Ellie came and sat beside me.

"This happens to me all the time."

"Do you think about King Leonidas as well?" I half-joked and smiled when Ellie put her arms around me and kissed me on the head.

"It's all right to be nervous. Even Spiro is nervous, isn't that right, Spiro?"

Mountain man Spiro looked back at us and nodded. He reminded me of a giant bear, and I doubted he feared anything. I wasn't convinced.

"You are prepared, Zoe. We are all ready, and we have the Lord on our side. We are fighting against flesh and blood, and we have a myriad of angels guiding us."

"I sure hope so."

"I know you are having a hard time sleeping. Why don't you sleep with me? I could use a cuddle." Ellie pulled me towards her and said something that I couldn't hear, but I'm sure it was a prayer to her God.

We went back inside the cave and lay down on the makeshift bed. Having Ellie's arms around me made me feel safe. The foreboding feelings that made my heart ache were still running through my mind, but I eventually felt myself slowly falling asleep.

* * *

It was time. I dressed in black, tied my hair back, and

covered my head with a black knit cap Mama had made for me. I checked and rechecked my crossbow and counted the arrows. I had made quite a few and stuck them in my quiver. I practiced taking one out, followed by another, and counted my time.

Ellie put her hand on my shoulder, and I looked up. Without a word, she dipped her fingers into a cup and brought the grease to my face. She reached into her pocket and took out a handgun. "Just in case you run out of arrows."

I merely nodded.

"I have one thing to say to you. Your job is to take out the driver and the soldier on the passenger side, and then keep firing until you can get on board and release the children. Your only job after that is to take them away from the battle and to bring them to the caves. Is that clear?"

"Yes."

"You and Stavros must not stop for anything. We will take care of the soldiers. You must save the children."

"I will run like the hounds of hell are after me."

Ellie nodded and went down on her haunches to draw in the dirt a Spartan shield with the lambda in the middle. I used to insist that the lambda stood for Lambros rather than Laconia. Ellie looked at me in all seriousness. "You're a warrior now."

She kissed my cheek before she walked away. The time had come for me to prove worthy of being in the Resistance. There was no going back.

With it or *on* it.

CHAPTER 32

I flattened myself on the ground in the tall grasses and waited. I was trying to say calm and focused, and the Hymn of Freedom kept repeating in my head. Ellie placed two bullets about a meter apart on flat rocks near me. When they fell over, it would signal the arrival of the trucks long before we heard them. I watched those bullets as if it was the second coming of Christ.

The first bullet fell over, and I prepared my crossbow. The second bullet fell over, and I was ready. Minutes later, the sound of trucks approaching signaled the time for doubt to end and my job to begin. I spotted the first truck heading my way. I quickly went through the steps I needed to take —fire my arrow through the windshield and hit the driver, and immediately follow that by shooting the second arrow and hitting the soldier in the passenger seat.

The closer it got, the more patient I needed to be. I had to fire at the right time. I waited as it approached and slowed down due to the debris on the road. The driver looked panicked for a moment and started to reverse the truck. I realized he had his door window down, which was even better for me. I stood up, rested on one knee, and fired my first arrow, which struck him in the neck. I had no time to think about that small victory. The truck veered dangerously close to the edge of the road and was about to slide off and into the gorge when the soldier in the passenger's seat took hold of the steering wheel. I got a good look at him as he came into view. I waited until he righted the truck and brought it back on the road, and then I fired the second arrow, and it struck him in the head. The vehicle hit debris and smashed into the mountainside.

The deaths of the two soldiers had a cascading effect when gunfire and screeching tires echoed in the valley. The front tire of the second vehicle blew out, followed by more shots. What we weren't expecting was the second truck to smash through the debris and push the first truck forward, so it ended up crashing the lorry into the mountainside.

The children! I had to release the children. I found myself further away from the first vehicle than I needed to be. I got up and started to run only to see more soldiers coming out of the first truck. Goddammit, they weren't supposed to be in that truck. I quickly loaded my crossbow and fired. I hit one of the soldiers in the shoulder and down he went, but my fourth arrow got stuck in my quiver. I pulled on it desperately as the second soldier approached with his gun drawn. He raised his weapon and was about to shoot me when he stumbled and then fell forward on the road. I turned to find Ellie right beside me. She didn't look like my cousin. There was this wild look in her eyes that I had never seen before. Her usually calm, sweet face had hardened to an angry snarl. An avenging angel. That's what she was—an angel that had just saved my life *again*. She went up to the wounded soldier and shot him in the head. That was the end of him.

"Go! Go! Go!" Ellie yelled at me as she ran to the other side of the road. There was another convoy of two trucks that would soon be coming around the bend. I was about to climb into the vehicle and open the back when someone from inside started shooting. Damnation! I narrowly escaped the bullets that struck the metal tailgate by flinging myself off the truck. I decided to slide under the truck and wait for whoever was shooting from inside to come out and confront me.

I was right. Moments later, I saw uniformed legs appear inches from my face as they jumped out from the back of the truck. I needed to come up with a plan to distract the soldier long enough for me to shoot him when I rolled out from under the vehicle. The attack wasn't going according to plan, but then I hadn't planned on sliding under a truck. I could exit from the right side, but I would be shot once the Germans caught sight of me. The other option was the back of the vehicle, but I needed a distraction so I could fire as soon as I came out. I slid further back while the soldiers outside were shooting at my comrades. It was fortunate I was petite because the little room I did have allowed me to load my crossbow. I had an idea of how I was going to get out, and if I pulled it off, it would let me get rid of the soldier standing in my way of the children. The soldier was wearing boots, but if I shot him through the ankle with my arrow, I would have time to get into position and then quickly load and fire my crossbow to finish the job.

The legs came closer, and I slid forward until he stood exactly where I wanted him to be. I brought the crossbow up and fired straight into his ankle. That had to hurt, and I smiled when he started to scream and curse. I took a deep breath and braced myself for what was to come. I would need to be ready to shoot as soon as I rolled out from under the vehicle. The soldier was hopping on one leg, trying to get the arrow out of his ankle and blindly firing his gun under the truck. The bullets flew harmlessly past me. I had seconds to slide out and shoot before he got lucky, and one of his shots would end my life.

Above me in the truck, the children were screaming in terror, and I couldn't wait any longer. I slid forward, and suddenly the tires bounced. Someone had jumped back on board. A trail of blood on the ground signaled it was my shot soldier.

I had the stomach-churning realization he was going to shoot the children rather than let them fall into the hands of the Resistance. I couldn't wait any longer. I rolled out from under the truck in an awkward position and realized the soldier was almost on top of me. He saw me, but he didn't have time to shoot because I fired my crossbow upside down. My arrow struck him in the chest, he took a few steps forward and then collapsed right over the edge of the truck and landed right next to me.

I lay on my back on the ground, my heart pounding against my chest and the dead soldier near my head. I was ready to pass out from pure terror when I felt a bullet whizz by and hit a tire. More bullets hit the truck and the ground beside me. I rolled away, and blindly fired an arrow. It hit the soldier who had been firing on me in the chest and out of the fight. Blind luck had killed him.

Just then, Stavros came rushing over. He had blood on his face and shirt. He looked at the two dead soldiers and patted me on the head, and then he hauled me up, and we boarded the truck.

To my amazement and disgust, there were about twenty terrified children in the back. "Get out of the truck!"

"I want my mama." That almost broke me because I wanted my mama as well, but neither of us was going to get what we wanted.

"I'll take you all to your mothers; come on, let's go!" I lied. Sometimes you have to tell a white lie, and this was one of those times.

Just as we got out, Stavros threw a stick grenade towards another group of soldiers that were running towards us. There were more soldiers than we had anticipated, but I didn't have time to worry about them. We herded the children through the thick brush and away from the fighting. We told them to run because we needed to get away from the Germans. They ran. Stavros was in the front, and I was in the back, herding the children. I almost stopped when I heard an explosion that was far too close, but I remembered Ellie telling me to run like the devil was after me.

"Stavros! Are you all right?" I yelled at him.

He didn't answer, but we kept on running for the caves. We reached them as more explosions echoed in the valley. Stavros took the children further into the caves, and I loaded my crossbow and sat at the mouth of the cave.

I took a deep breath and noticed my hands were

shaking. I tried to stand, but my knees trembled, so I decided sitting was the better choice. I sat back against the cave wall, and I took in great gulps of air. I got into a position to fire my crossbow when I heard movement headed my way. I was feeling quite sick, but I was going to defend the children with my life if I had to.

"Zoe! Don't shoot; it's us!"

I dropped my crossbow in relief and couldn't get up fast enough to embrace Ellie with all my might. Behind her was a group of women, and behind them came the rest of the Resistance cell.

Ellie put her arm around my shoulders and leaned in. "I saw you roll out from under the truck. Impressive upside-down shooting, ZoZo!"

"I bet Laskarina didn't do that!"

We laughed as we trudged our way into the cave. Ellie let go of me to usher the women inside, and I remained at the entrance. Giorgos also stayed, and we guarded the cave together. I could see the fires from the burning trucks light up the night.

Ellie put her arm around me and kissed me on the head. "He was killed by a Spartan girl! I bet he is going to get reminded of that for eternity while he is roasting in hell."

I had survived my first battle, slightly dented but still alive.

I was going home 'with it' rather than 'on it.'

CHAPTER 33

I should have been tired, but there was too much energy running through my veins. Every time I shut my eyes, I could see the German soldier's blue eyes looking into mine. He wasn't much older than me. Was it terror? Was it hatred? I don't know, but I didn't want to see his face, so I tried to stay awake.

I wasn't sure why we didn't just leave the cave and rendezvous with the other team that was waiting on the other side of the mountain. I glanced towards Ellie. I wondered if she could read my thoughts because she smiled and came towards me.

"Are you a mind reader?"

Ellie chuckled and sat down next to me. "You're not that hard to read, ZoZo. You're fidgeting and not getting the rest I told you to get. You want to get out of here."

"I do. Why haven't we left?"

"We're waiting on two teams to come back."

"Shouldn't they be here already?"

Ellie paused for a moment and then nodded. "Yes."

"Does that mean something has happened to them?" What a stupid question. Of course, something had happened; that's why they were late. I do ask ridiculous questions sometimes.

"Never stop questioning, because if you stop, you will never learn."

I wasn't sure what to say about that because most people told me not to ask so many questions. "What does it mean that they are late?"

"We will find out when they get here."

Giorgos called out to Ellie that we had company. Ellie left my side and joined him at the cave entrance.

I expected the worst and had my crossbow at the ready, but I shouldn't have worried. Uncle Petros, Apostolos, and two other men ran in. Ellie put her arms around her father, and they stood there for a long moment. If someone had asked me if Ellie had been worried about the team's delayed return, I would have said no. She clung on to her father, and it was clear that it was a relief.

I was a little jealous... I wished to be hugging my father at that moment. I slapped myself on the head for being so stupid. "Ow," I muttered and hoped no one had seen what I had done. I went over to my uncle and gave him a hug trying not to think of my irrational jealous moment.

I caught sight of Apostolos and mentally rolled my eyes because he was giving me a look that I couldn't decipher. What did that boy want! I turned away and went back to my little corner of the cave.

After Ellie finished speaking to her father and the rest

of the team, she came over and sat beside me. She just stared at me. "What?"

"Go and talk to him."

"Why?"

Ellie was having far too much fun at my expense. I glanced at Apostolos, who sat just a little further away from me and let out a low growl that had Ellie laughing. That wasn't my intention. Ellie fell back against the cave wall and laughed. "Oh, Zoe, I love you, but you are adorable when you're clueless."

"I don't want to marry him."

"No one is forcing you to marry him now. You're too young. When you get to sixteen, then you two will make a beautiful couple."

I almost gagged at the thought. I stopped myself from saying, 'why don't you marry him?' At least I'm not an insensitive imbecile all the time.

"He's just come back from battle, and he wants to talk to someone."

"Where do you think I was? I wasn't baking bread."

Ellie's obvious amusement made me smile. It was good for her to laugh, and if I was the butt of the joke, I didn't mind. "Yeah, but it was a little dicey so that he might want a little…"

I stared incredulously at her. I leaned in and whispered, "Are you asking me to go over there and kiss him?"

"Heavens, no! Just talk to him."

I sighed. "When are we leaving?"

"Soon. We're waiting for our trucks to arrive so they can take our precious cargo. Once they do, that team will handle their rescue from there."

"Dawn is nearly here; won't it be too late if we delay?"

"We have a few more hours before daybreak," Ellie reassured me and glanced at Apostolos again. "You and he would make such beautiful babies. With his hair and your eyes..."

I slapped my cousin on the head, which only made her laugh harder. I loved watching her laugh because it made me feel good. She was still chuckling when she left me.

It didn't take Apostolos long to make his way over. I wanted to move, but that would have been rude, even for me. He sat down and let his head fall back and looked up into the cave wall. I rolled my eyes. What was he trying to do?

"Zo..."

"Zoe," I corrected him. Only my family called me 'Zo' or 'ZoZo.'

"Miss Lambros..."

"Oh, dear God," I muttered. He wasn't a young boy, but he acted like one. What kind of fool doesn't look you in the eye, especially when he was trying to impress me? "What do you want, Toli?"

Have you ever seen a puppy when you're playing with them? They wag their tail, and they have a happy look on their faces. If Apostolos had been a dog, then his big blue eyes would have been round with happiness, and his tail would have been spinning at dizzying speed. It didn't take much to make him happy. I had only used his nickname. I hadn't agreed to marry him. "Is this how all men are? God help me," I thought.

"I know it's not the right time to talk to you about this..."

He was not going to ask me to marry him, was he? Hopefully, I wasn't going to end up shooting him, because I still had my gun. It was loaded and ready.

"I don't want to marry you."

"Oh, I know that."

Oh, good, he wasn't a complete idiot.

"I didn't mean we should get married now. You're too young, and you know, young and young…"

What? What was he babbling on about?

"When you're older, then we can get married as your father promised."

He was still talking, and for the first time, I thought ill of my father. How could he promise me in marriage to an Athenian with crazy blue eyes and that stupid accent of his? What was my father thinking! Must have been the anxiety about the war. That had to be it.

"Don't you find it old-fashioned to be promised in marriage?" *Please, say yes, please.*

"No. It's a great tradition. That's how my parents got married."

Of course, they did. Oh, God, spare me, I'm sorry I called you names. Save me. When I was losing hope, I remembered something.

"I don't have a dowry."

"You have all the fields your father left you, and your brothers' fields and houses."

Damn. I had forgotten about the fields. "Do you want to marry me for my money?"

Apostolos laughed, and all I wanted to do was slap him. "I have more than enough money to keep you in luxury.

You will be my queen with servants and everything you want."

Keep me in luxury? KEEP ME? Ugh.

"I know it will take some time for you to love me, but it will happen. I can wait."

I was going to be dismissive of his opinion, but he was honest. I could see it in his eyes. I believed him. "Toli, I'm not ready to marry you."

"Oh, no, not now! When you turn sixteen. We will have a huge wedding, and everyone will dance and sing."

"Not even then."

"You say that now because you're not ready, but I will prove to you how much I love you."

I had never had any boys give me their undying love before. What was I supposed to do with that? I was about to tell him again that I wasn't going to be ready at sixteen either when I saw Ellie approaching. Gone were the smiles and the relaxed woman I had seen only thirty minutes before.

She went down on her haunches and touched my hand. "I want you to get up and go with Stavros, Apostolos, and Giorgos. The cave has another exit, but it will take you some time to get out. You are to go through the caves with our guests."

"I thought we were waiting on—"

"We're not. Dimitri went further down the path, looking for the truck. The Germans found them. We need to get the women and children out of here."

"You're not coming with us?"

"No. I'm staying with my father and the rest of the men."

"What are you defending? Piles of rocks? I'm staying with you." I was getting more than a little angry at this new arrangement.

Ellie put her hands on either side of my shoulders. "I'm giving you an order. Your mission is to save those women and children."

I could see the frustration in her eyes. I could see she wanted to yell at me to follow orders like a good soldier, but she didn't give voice to her frustration. "One of the women in that group is an important member of the Resistance. If the Germans find out who she is, our whole Resistance mission is in jeopardy…it's important, Zoe. Do you understand?"

"I understand, but why did we wait so long?"

"That wasn't the plan."

"Well, it's the plan now. Let's all leave. We can all escape together."

"We can't. When the Germans find the cave empty, they will enter and follow us."

"Or they could say no one is here and move on."

"We can't let the Germans capture this woman. She was already in their grasp, and they didn't know who she is then. You need to obey orders."

"I'm going to, but how do we know that the Germans won't be waiting for us when we get out?"

"You don't know, but there's no reason they should be there."

"That's reassuring," I replied sarcastically.

Ellie grimaced and took off her gold chain with her wedding band that hung around her neck. She took my hand and placed the chain on it. "I'll come over to the farm, and you can give this back to me."

"You promise? A promise is a promise, Elisavet."

"I promise. Now get going."

She was lying to me. We both knew she was lying. I hugged her and held on for longer than I should have. I didn't want to leave her. My heart was screaming at me to stay, but I had to go. I was a soldier and had to obey orders.

We rounded the women and children and headed further into the caves. I stopped before joining them and looked back. My cousin, my sister, my best friend — stood tall and brave, the fierce warrior I had witnessed in battle. I saluted her while my heart shattered into a million pieces. Ellie acknowledged my salute. We stood there for a long moment before she pointed to the retreating Jewish women and children and mouthed, 'Be brave like Laskarina. I love you.'

Did the Spartans cry as they left King Leonidas to face the mighty Persians with just three hundred men? I doubt they wept for their king because they were mighty warriors. I was abandoning Ellie to withstand demonic forces and crying bitter, angry tears that rolled down my cheeks as I ran to catch up with the rest of the team.

I hated God. I hated him with all my heart.

CHAPTER 34

We ran through the caves as the sound of gunfire echoed behind us. The Germans had indeed arrived. I wanted to go back and fight with them, but I had a mission to complete. To our relief, there were no Germans on the other side of the cave, and we ran out. Waiting for us were villagers willing to help us evade the Germans. We had horses and wagons, and we loaded everyone on them and set them on their way with another group of men.

Our job was done, and I was ready to head back, but Stavros hulled me back by pulling on my jacket. "What in the hell are you doing?" I screamed at him. "I'm going back!"

"NO!" Stavros pushed me away and pointed to the caves we had to reach on the other side of the mountain. "Move!" he screamed at me and shoved me away from the entrance of the cave we had just come through.

Reluctantly, I ran away and followed the rest of the group, all the while cursing Stavros and God. Daylight was fast approaching, and any efforts we had made to hide from the Germans were going to come to naught if we were spotted. We ran into the caves, and I collapsed in a heap. My heart was beating so fast it made me breathless, and I clutched my chest.

I wanted to take the gun I had in my waistband and shoot Stavros for leaving his family behind. He had abandoned them in their time of need, and that was unforgivable. It was worse than being a traitor. I couldn't take the 'sitting around doing nothing' part of the mission.

"We have to go back!"

"No," Stavros said quietly from where he had been sitting at the mouth of the cave. "No, we can't."

"Stav, our family… YOUR FAMILY!"

"We can't go back to save them." His voice broke with emotion, but I was not ready to forgive him for betrayal. His father and his sister had been slaughtered, and there was nothing we could do other than sit in a godforsaken cave. We sat in that cave for hours until Stavros and Apostolos got up and armed themselves.

"You're going back? I'm coming with you." I slung my crossbow across my back and was ready to go out with them until Stavros turned and put his arm on my shoulder.

"We are, but you're not. You're staying here."

"No," I replied vehemently. "I'm coming with you."

"I won't let you."

"Dammit, Stav…"

"What happens if there are Germans still around?"

"We shoot them dead. What would you do if there are Germans around? Invite them to dinner? I want to bring them home, and—"

"Zoe, for once in your life, will you just listen to me and stop arguing?" Stavros's patience with me had evaporated. "You can't go into that cave again. We don't know what we will find, but I know what those demons do to the Resistance. I will not allow you to see that."

"You have no right to tell me what I can or can't do!"

"LISTEN TO ME! I AM THE HEAD OF THIS FAMILY!" Stavros screamed in my face, and his spittle landed on my face. "I am the head. My father and sister are dead. Don't you think I wanted to go in there and rescue them? Goddammit, Zoe!"

"Stav…you left them to die."

"I KNOW I DID!" Stavros pushed me aside and was about to walk out of the cave when he stopped and looked back. "I don't want another Mavrakis to die tonight. I also don't want you to remember… just stay here; it's an order. Obey it like you would have if it were Ellie who had given you the orders instead of me."

The waiting was excruciating, but I followed my orders despite wanting to disobey and run after them. It was close to midnight when Stavros and Apostolos returned along with a group of villagers and their wagon. I didn't want to see what was in the cart. I didn't want that last image of my beloved family to be seared into my mind. Stavros had been right. I also didn't blame Ellie for the choice she had made, but the thought did cross my mind that she had wanted to die and be with her beloved Angelos. I had never had a love that consumed my mind and heart as Ellie had for Angelos. It had to be so powerful that you could think of nothing else.

We made our way back to Farsala under the cover of darkness. We had been successful in rescuing the women and children, but we had paid a heavy price for that victory.

We were bringing our fallen heroes *on* their shields.

CHAPTER 35

MAY 20, 1942

FARSALA / ATHENA'S BLUFF

I like Spring. I love the flowers and the warmth it brings, although the heat had decided not to make an appearance today. I rode my bicycle down the road leading to the grove feeling proud of myself. The Italians were in an uproar because the Resistance had killed Busto. I had to hide my joy because, as my mother reminded me, I shouldn't rejoice when someone died, but, in this case, I was thrilled that I had been part of that mission.

Ellie had been right that I was perfect for the surveillance of Busto's house. I had observed his routine, and I had even managed to get into the house on multiple occasions. I was a harmless child doing some chores. They were oblivious to the danger. I did get my first look at the Nazi Bonhoffen and hoped I wasn't going to see him again.

I passed an Italian patrol and gave them a wide berth,

but their attention wasn't on me. I had a few things to do today, and they all involved visiting the cemetery and then Athena's Bluff. Mama and I were going to stay up there tonight because our farm was being used to hide Allied soldiers.

I got off my bicycle and opened the gate leading to the cemetery. I leaned the bike against the gnarly tree and entered. My father's grave had weeds growing around it. I had been so busy with the Resistance activities that I hadn't plucked the weeds. I picked them out and took out my drawing of Mama and myself. The overwhelming sadness I had been keeping at bay from this morning washed over me. I knelt beside the grave and buried the artwork.

"Happy birthday, Papa. I wish you were here. So much has happened. I'm sure Ellie and Uncle Petros will have told you by now..." I couldn't continue because the tears rolled down my face, and all I could do was cry.

I wiped my eyes and kissed the headstone before I moved away because I couldn't stay the night like I wanted to. My mama needed me. I approached Ellie's grave, and I took out the ring that she had given me. I was forbidden to see Ellie's body. Had I had the opportunity to see her before she was buried, I would have placed the chain around her neck. We both knew why she gave me her ring. She was giving up her life to save another and wanted me to keep the symbol of her love. She knew what I would do with it.

What did Father H say when we brought our heroes back? 'Greater love has no one than this: to lay down one's life for one's friends.' And that is what my beloved father, uncle, and my cousin had done—they had died saving others. Could I live up to that heroism?

Father H had conducted the funeral, and I wasn't sure what it meant for a Jewish person to be buried like a Christian, but I was sure her God would understand. We had a Jewish family stay in our cellar for a few days. Sara was my age, and I asked her how Jewish people mourned their dead. I also wanted to know all about the Jews and why this was happening to them, and Sara was willing to answer my questions, but there were some things she didn't know. Soon after Ellie's funeral, I came out to the grove and sat shiva for her, just as Sara had told me. I celebrated Ellie's life, and I lit a small candle I had, but I couldn't leave it lit as Sara said it had to be done. I think Ellie would have liked that. I knelt and buried the ring as far as I could push it into the soil.

I sat down between the two graves and looked up into the trees. "It's Spring, and so much has happened. I have some good news, Ellie. First, I have to tell you that you were right. My mission to monitor troops was perfect for me. Busto is dead, long may he fry in hell." I looked around me as a slight breeze picked up, and the warmth touched my face. "You were also right about the Germans. I see more of them in Larissa than there used to be. It might have something to do with Busto going boom, but I think something else is going on. We did get a new commander, but he's not Italian. Stavros tells me he's a Nazi SS officer."

I hoped I was genuinely alone because talking about Busto's death was something that could quickly get me killed if it was overheard.

"Mama says that killing Busto will only result in another monster assigned to Larissa. We weren't expecting the Nazis. I'm not sure why this has happened, but it doesn't matter. We will kill him too. They can send as many monsters as they like; we will kill them all."

I glanced at my watch and sighed. I couldn't stay for very long because of the curfew, and the last thing I wanted on my father's birthday was to tangle with a patrol. I stood up and dusted the soil from my pants. I glanced at the sack that lay next to my feet and smiled.

"Before I go, I want to tell you what happened a few nights ago. Stavros and Apostolos raided a convoy. Stavros is worried about me, and he tries not to get me involved, which is annoying. I was in the same battle he was at Lamia, but he still doesn't want me to go with him. It doesn't matter what Stavros wants. They brought back a crate of dynamite. That's when I had an idea."

I giggled at the ingenious plan I had concocted because it fulfilled a promise I had made to Ellie. I always keep my word. "Yesterday, I went to the traitor's grave. Yes, I know what you're going to say, but a promise is a promise. I took four sticks of dynamite and buried them in his grave. There are some days I get some excellent ideas. I lit the dynamite, and it went boom! It was a sight, Ellie! Dirt and body parts flew everywhere!" I laughed and felt silly at clapping my hands at my plan, but it didn't matter.

"The Italians came running because it wasn't far from one of their bases. The thought did cross my mind that I could pick them off as they came to the exploded grave, but there were too many of them. They all appeared to be a little perplexed about why someone would bomb a grave. I laughed so much watching the fools. After they left, I went back and found the head. Luckily it had landed in the brushes. That's what I have in the sack. I told you that I was going to take that fat bastard up the mountain and burn him. A promise is a promise."

With a heavy sigh, I picked up the sack, flung it over my shoulder, and walked out of the cemetery. "Come on, Uncle Traitorous Pig. It's going to be lovely up the mountain." I giggled as I rode my bicycle towards Athena's Bluff and reached it before the curfew.

I got off the bike and walked up the path leading to the cabin. For a moment, I stood there and remembered that night with Ellie. I deliberately dragged the sack over every rock and hit every tree trunk going up.

"Zoe! I was getting worried you wouldn't get here in time!"

Mama came out of the cabin and put her arms around me. "Did you bury your drawing?"

"I did."

Mama tilted my head up and gazed at me. "You've been crying."

"One of these days, Mama, I'm going to run out of tears."

"I know." Mama held me for a long moment. "I made some rabbit stew."

I looked up at her in surprise. "You killed a rabbit?"

"Stavros killed it." Mama laughed. "Ah, vegetables, is that what's in the sack?"

"You won't like…" Mama reached out and took hold of the sack. It wasn't the vegetables she was expecting. The look on her face when she saw what was in it almost made me want to laugh. I tried hard not to laugh but couldn't help myself.

"Zoe Lambros! My dear God, child, what have you

done?"

"I've fulfilled a promise I made to Ellie. I told her I was going to carry this fat bast...er...fat pig up the mountain and throw him off Athena's Bluff for betraying Angelos."

Mama turned away and headed back inside the cabin. "I don't want to know how you managed to get that head."

"It was easy; I—"

"I don't want to know."

I smiled. Mama had a gentle heart. I created a fire pit and brought out the head of the traitor. There were bits of him missing. At least now he wasn't fat. I spat on what was left of his face and then lit the fire.

Unfortunately, the fire wasn't that hot, so it wouldn't turn the skull to ashes. I took away the fire pit and lined up the head like a footballer about to shoot for goal. I looked up to find Stavros watching me from the doorway.

"Zoe, have you ever thought you might not be sane?"

"No, that never entered my mind," I replied and went back to aligning the head with Mount Ossa in the background.

"You won't be able to kick it. You're going to hurt your foot if you do."

I looked down at my sandal-covered feet, and I had to admit Stavros was right. I had a brilliant idea. I took the skull out of the fire pit and placed it on the outcrop. I went back to where my bicycle was and took out my crossbow from my bag. Stavros laughed when he figured out what I was going to do and sat down on the bench outside. I loaded my crossbow and positioned myself on the ground. I fired the arrow, and it hit the skull, sending it flying over the edge of the lookout and down into the gorge. I went over to the lookout and watched its descent. I lifted my crossbow in triumph and danced a little jig.

I stood on the precipice and gazed across the now darkened valley. One year of occupation had passed, a year of death and misery but also of resistance, strength and courage. I lost my father, beloved cousins Ellie, Angelos and Arty, uncles Petros and Ignatius and so many of my extended family and friends to the invaders. Their courage in the face of evil strengthened my resolve to continue my mission to rid the vermin occupying my country and to help our Jewish friends and Allies.

With it or *On* it.

Freedom or death.

I will resist and fight until my last breath.

THE END

Read more of Zoe's story in the novel
"In The Blood of the Greeks"

Thank you for taking the time to read "Enemy at the Gate". If you enjoyed it, please consider telling your friends or posting a short review from the store you purchased this novel. Word of mouth is an author's best friend and much appreciated.

Thank you,
Mary

HISTORICAL REFERENCES IN THE NOVEL

With all my stories, I embed real history into the fictional story. Such is the case with this novel "Enemy at the Gate" – Here are some of the historical references of people, places and events from the story with links to get more information about the event.

CHAPTER 1 – EARTHQUAKE IN LARISSA MARCH 01, 1941

At 5:55 am on March 01, 1941 Larissa experienced a devastating earthquake that measured 6.3 on the Richter Scale. It was so powerful that more than 19,000 out of 24,000 inhabitants were left homeless. 10,000 of the houses that collapsed were uninhabitable. The Royal Air Force bombers carried heavy loads of medical and other supplies from Athens to the stricken city over the coming days. Singleton Argus (NSW, Australia) - March 03, 1941
https://trove.nla.gov.au/newspaper/article/81977611

CHAPTER 3 ITALIAN BOMBING OF LARISSA - MARCH 02-04, 1941

In the early hours of March 02, 1941, Larissa was attacked from the air by Italian planes that dropped bombs for half an hour on the earthquake-stricken inhabitants of Larissa. Due to the earthquake the previous day, the inhabitants had no shelter from the bombs. The Italians continued the bombing raids for several more days.

Newspaper reports:
The Daily News (Perth, Western Australia) – March 3, 1941
https://trove.nla.gov.au/newspaper/article/78819544/8197949

CHAPTER 8-9
THE BATTLE OF TEMPE GORGE - APRIL 16-18, 1941

Tempe Gorge, on the eastern coast of Greece, was the site of a rear-guard action fought by Australian and New Zealand troops on 16-18 April 1941. The gorge is formed where the Pinios River, on its way to the sea, cuts through the coastal mountain range, to the south-east of Mount Olympus. Its name is derived from the village of Tempe that stands at its western end. In 1941, both a railway and road used the gorge to cross inland from the coast and connect with the town of Larissa. Larissa was a vital junction at which several other roads and railways converged and through which British and Commonwealth forces retreating from northern Greece had to pass. To protect Larissa long enough for this to occur, the 16th Australian Brigade, minus the 2/1st Battalion, but with the 21st New Zealand Battalion under its command, was deployed to prevent German movement through the gorge. The defenders took up positions on the slopes to the south - the New Zealanders overlooking the gorge itself and the

2/2nd and 2/3rd Battalions covering the western end where it opened onto a plain known as the Vale of Tempe.

The Germans launched a two-pronged attack on the morning of 18 April. Troops from the 2nd Armored Division attacked along the gorge from the east, while two regiments of the 6th Mountain Division that had moved through the mountains attacked from the north towards the Vale of Tempe. By midday, the New Zealanders had been forced to yield the gorge to Germans and withdrew in scattered parties, either across the hills to the south or through the 2/2nd Battalion's positions.

A lull in the fighting occurred for a few hours before the Germans renewed their attack on the 2/2nd mid-afternoon. Attacks from across the river were beaten off but the resolute drive of the German armor down the road, combined with a German outflanking movement to the west that was assisted by the premature withdrawal of part of the 2/3rd Battalion, brought about the collapse of the 2/2nd's position. After 6 pm its withdrew in parties of varying sizes across the hills to the south, with German troops in close pursuit; the battalion never fought as a whole again for the rest of the campaign.

In the hours after the capture of Tempe Gorge, the 2/3rd Battalion, a company of the 2/2nd, and a mixed group of other Australian and New Zealand troops fought as a mobile rear-guard down the road towards Larissa, sometimes engaging the German tanks at almost point-blank range. By dawn this force had been scattered and outflanked, but the primary withdrawal through Larissa had been completed without incident.

Source: The Australian War Memorial: https://www.awm.gov.au/collection/E84364

CHAPTER 12
KRISTALLNACHT - NOVEMBER 9-10, 1938

Kristallnacht or the Night of Broken Glass, was a coordinated attack against Jews by the paramilitary forces called Sturmabteilung (also known as the 'Brown Shirts') and civilians throughout Nazi Germany from November 9-10, 1938. The German authorities including police and firemen, looked on without intervening.

The name Kristallnacht ("Crystal Night") comes from the shards of broken glass that littered the streets after the windows of Jewish-owned stores, buildings and synagogues were smashed. Jewish homes, hospitals and schools were ransacked as the attackers demolished buildings with sledgehammers.

The rioters destroyed 267 synagogues throughout Germany, Austria and the Sudetenland. Over 7,000 Jewish businesses were damaged or destroyed, and 30,000 Jewish men were arrested and incarcerated in concentration camps.

The pretext for the attacks was the assassination of the Nazi diplomat Ernst vom Rath by Herschel Grynszpan, a 17-year-old German-born Polish Jew living in Paris. Estimates of fatalities caused by the attacks have varied. Early reports estimated that 91 Jews had been murdered but that was incorrect and it has been estimated that it was in the hundreds.

Kristallnacht is viewed as the prelude to the Final Solution and the murder of six million Jews during the Holocaust.

Find out more here: https://www.yadvashem.org/yv/en/exhibitions/kristallnacht/index.asp

CHAPTER 12
THE HOLOCAUST IN GREECE & THE RESISTANCE
1941 TO 1945

During World War II, when Greece was occupied by Nazi Germany, 86% of the Greek Jews, especially those in the areas occupied by Nazi Germany and Bulgaria, were massacred despite efforts by the Greek Orthodox Church and many Christian Greeks to shelter Jews. Although the Nazis deported numerous Greek Jews, many were hidden by their Greek neighbors. Roughly 49,000 Jews – Romaniotes and Sephardim – were deported from Thessaloniki alone and murdered.

Of its pre-occupation population of 72,000, only 12,000 survived, either by joining the resistance or being hidden. Most of those who died were deported to Auschwitz, while those in Thrace, under Bulgarian occupation, were sent to Treblinka.

The Italians did not deport Jews living in the territory they controlled, but when the Germans took over, Jews living there were also deported (Larissa was under Italian rule until the Germans came and then the Germans began their murderous rampage of Jews in Larissa).

After the war, a majority of the survivors emigrated to Israel, the United States, and Western Europe. Today there are still functioning Romaniote Synagogues in Chalkis which represents the oldest Jewish congregation on European ground, in Ioannina, Athens, New York and Israel.

Find out more here: The Jewish Museum of Greece https://www.jewishmuseum.gr/en/welcome-to-the-jewish-museum-of-greece/

CHAPTER 24
BOUBOULINA RESISTANCE GROUP

Eleni "Lela" Karagianni, her husband and her seven children lived in Athens in 1941. When Greece surrendered in 1941, the city was occupied by the Germans. Eleni, her husband and her older sons soon joined the National Republican Greek League (EDES) resistance group. Eleni soon formed her own cell into the broader movement and called it the 'Bouboulinas'.

The name came from the legendary Greek Captain **Laskarina Bouboulina** (11 May 1771 – 22 May 1825) was a Greek naval commander, heroine of the Greek War of Independence in 1821. Karagianni and her fellow partisans operated out of her husband's pharmacy in Athens and from a monastery in Megara. The cell distributed information to other cells, smuggled wanted individuals into areas controlled by Greek partisan forces, and forged documents, and coordinated with British military intelligence to disrupt the Axis occupation. It also helped Allied soldiers and Jews escape the Italian and Germans.

In July 1944, Karagianni was arrested in Athens by the Germans and taken to the SS headquarters where she was tortured before being sent to the Haidari concentration camp on the outskirts of Athens. While at the concentration camp, Elena continued to coordinate a resistance effort against the Germans. On September 08, 1944, only two weeks before Athens was liberated, Eleni Karagianni was executed by firing squad.

On September 13, 2011 Yad Vashem recognized Eleni "Lela" Karagianni as Righteous among the Nations. Lela was given that honor for saving the Solomon Cohen family. It was April 1944 when Solomon Cohen, his wife Regina and their young daughter Shelley knocked at Karagiannis' door. She gave them her help even though the Germans were already suspicious of her having taken part in acts of resistance. Lela also made sure the family was taken to a safe hideout when the situation deteriorated further.

Read more about Eleni here:
https://en.wikipedia.org/wiki/Lela_Karagianni

List of Greek Resistance Groups
https://en.wikipedia.org/wiki/Greek_Resistance

ABOUT MARY

Mary is an award-winning author of historical fiction, romance and urban fantasy stories. Mary works as a graphic and web designer - creating art for her colouring books and designing web sites. Mary has won numerous awards for her fiction, but one of the highlights of her life (and one of the biggest thrills) was to have her first novel "In the Blood of the Greeks" and the non-fiction "In the Blood of the Greeks: The Illustrated Companion" showcased in the Jewish Museum of Greece's book collection about the holocaust in Greece during WW2. Mary lives in Australia and when she's not writing, creating art or designing sites, she is a voracious reader of historical novels (especially those set during WW1 and WW2) and murder mysteries!

Newsletter
http://eepurl.com/-5USD

Official Site
http://www.nextchapter.net

On Social Media:
Facebook: http://facebook.com/marydbrooksfiction
Twitter: http://twitter.com/marydbrooksfic
Instagram: http://instagram.com/ausxipmaryd

OTHER NOVELS BY MARY

Shorts

Short 1: Horns and Halos

Short 2: Crossroads

Standalone Novels in the Eva and Zoe Universe

Novella: A Widgie Knight

Novella: Zoe's Promise

Novel: Mabel of the ANZACS

Intertwined Souls Series – Eva and Zoe

Book 1: In The Blood of the Greeks

Book 2: Where Shadows Linger

Book 3: Hidden Truths

Book 4: Awakenings Book 5: No Good Deed

Book 5: No Good Deed

Book 6: Nor The Battle To The Strong

Non-Fiction

In the Blood of the Greeks The Illustrated Companion